Letters from my Windmill

Letters from my Windmill

by Alphonse Daudet

©2012 SMK Books

Wilder Publications, LLC.
PO Box 3005
Radford VA 24143-3005

ISBN 10: 1-61720-717-9
ISBN 13: 978-1-61720-717-4

Table of Contents:

Foreword

As witnessed by Master Honorat Grapazi, lawyer at the residence of Pampérigouste.

"As summoned

"Mr Gaspard Mitifio, husband of Vivette Cornille, tenant at the place called Les Cigalières and resident there.

"Who herewith has sold and transferred under guarantee by law and deed and free of all debts, privileges and mortgages,

"To Mr Alphonse Daudet, poet, living in Paris, here present and accepting it.

"A windmill and flourmill, located in the Rhône valley, in the heart of Provence, on a wooded hillside of pines and green oaks; being the said windmill, abandoned for over twenty years, and not viable for grinding, as it appears that wild vines, moss, rosemary, and other parasitic greenery are climbing up to the sails;

"Notwithstanding the condition it is in and performs, with its grinding wheel broken, its platform brickwork grown through with grass, this affirms that the Mr Daudet finds the said windmill to his liking and able to serve as a workplace for his poetry, and accepts it whatever the risk and danger, and without any recourse to the vendor for any repairs needing to be made thereto.

"This sale has taken place outright for the agreed price, that the Mr Daudet, poet, has put and deposed as a type of payment, which price has been redeemed and received by the Mr Mitifio, all the foregoing having been seen by the lawyers and the undersigned witnesses, whose bills are to be confirmed.

"Deed made at Pampérigouste, in Honorat's office, in the presence of Francet Mamaï, fife player, and of Louiset, known as Quique, crucifix carrier for the white penitents;

"Who have signed, together with the parties above and the lawyer after reading it."

First Impressions

I am not sure who was the more surprised when I arrived—me or the rabbits.... The door had been bolted and barred for a long time, and the walls and platform were overgrown with weeds; so, understandably, the rabbits had come to the conclusion that millers were a dying breed. They had found the place much to their liking, and felt fully entitled to made the windmill their general and strategic headquarters. The night I moved in, I tell you, there were over twenty of them, sprawled around the apron, basking in the moonlight. When I opened a window, the whole encampment scampered off, their white scuts bobbing up and down until they had completely disappeared into the brush. I do hope they come back, though.

Another much surprised resident was also not best comforted by my arrival. It was the old, thoughtful, sinister-looking owl, a sitting tenant for some twenty years. I found him stiff and motionless on his roost of fallen plaster and tiles. He ran his large round eyes over me briefly and then, probably much put out by the presence of a stranger, he hooted, and painfully and carefully shook his dusty, grey wings;—they ponder too much these owlish, thinking types and never keep themselves clean ... it didn't matter! even with his blinking eyes and his sullen expression, this particular occupant would suit me better than most, and I immediately decided he was only too welcome to stay. He stayed right there, just where he'd always been, at the very top of the mill near his own personal roof entrance. Me—I settled down below in a little, whitewashed, vaulted, and low-ceilinged room, much like a nun's refectory.

I am writing to you from my windmill, with the door wide open to the brilliant sunshine.

In front of me, a lovely, sparklingly lit, pine wood plunges down to the bottom of the hill. The nearest mountains, the Alpilles, are far away, their grand silhouettes pressing against the sky.... There was hardly a sound to be heard; a fading fife, a curlew calling amongst the lavender, and a tinkle of mules' bells from somewhere along the track. The Provencal light really brings this beautiful landscape to life.

Don't you wonder, right now, if I am missing your black and bustling Paris? Actually, I'm very contented in my windmill; it is just the sort of warm, sweet-smelling spot I was looking for, a long, long way from newspapers, hansom cabs, and all that fog!... Also, I am surrounded by so many lovely things. My head is bursting with vivid memories and wonderful impressions, after only eight days here. For instance, yesterday evening, I saw the flocks of animals returning from the hills to the farm (the mas), and I swear that I wouldn't swap this one hillside wonder for a whole week's worth of Premieres in Paris. Well, I'll let you be the judge.

Here in Provence, it's normal practice to send the sheep into the mountains when it's warm enough in the spring, and, for five or six months, man and beast live together with nothing but the sky for a roof and grass for a bed. When the first autumn chill is felt in the air, they are brought back down to the mas, and they can graze comfortably on the nearby rose-mary-scented hills.... This annual delight, the return of the flock, was accomplished last night. The double barn doors had been left expectantly open since daybreak and the barn had already been covered with fresh straw. There was occasional, excited speculation about the flock's exact where-abouts; "Now they are in Eyguières" or "They are in Paradou" was rumoured. Then suddenly, towards evening, we heard a rousing shout of "Here they come" and we could see the magnificent cloud of dust that heralded the approach of the flock. As it continued along its way, it seemed to gather everything into its path to join the great march home.... The old rams, horns assertively pointing forward, lead the way, with the rest of the sheep behind; the ewes looked tired out, with their new-born lambs getting under their feet;—Mules bedecked with red pom-poms were carrying day-old lambs in baskets and rocking them to sleep with a gentle motion. Then came the breathless, overworked dogs, tongues hanging out, in the company of two strapping shepherds in their red serge, ground-hugging cloaks.

The whole parade filed merrily past before being swallowed up by the open barn doors. They shuffled inside with a noise like a tropical downpour.... You should have seen the turmoil inside. The huge, silken tulle-crested, green and gold peacocks loudly trumpeted their welcome as they recognised the new arrivals. The early-to-bed hens scattered everywhere as they were woken up. All the pigeons, ducks, turkeys, and guinea-fowl were running or flying wildly about. The whole poultry yard was going absolutely mad!... You'd think that every single sheep had brought back an intoxicating dose of wild mountain air in its fleece, which had made all the other animals hopping mad.

In the midst of all this commotion, the flock somehow managed to settle themselves in. You couldn't imagine anything more charming than this homecoming. The old rams relaxed visibly at the sight of their home farm, while the tiny lambs born during the descent looked all around in astonished wonder.

But, it was the dogs that were the most touching, the gentle sheep dogs, who had busily looked after their charges until they were all safely back in the farm. The guard dog, barking from his kennel, did his best to call them over, and the well-bucket, brimming over with cool water, also competed to tempt them. But nothing, nothing could distract them, at least not until the livestock were all safely inside the pen, the small gate securely latched by its large bolt, and the shepherds seated at the table of their low-ceilinged room. Only then were they content to go to their dog pound, lap up their slop, and spread the news to the other animals, of the adventures they had had in the mountains—that mysterious world of wolves, and tall, purple foxgloves brimming over with dew.

The Coach from Beaucaire

I took the coach from Beaucaire to get to my windmill. It was a good old patache, a sort of rural coach, which, although it only made short trips, dawdled so much that by the end of the day it had the wearied air of having travelled a long way. There were five of us on top, plus the driver of course.

There was a thick-set, hairy, and earthy-smelling Camargue Ranger, with big, blood-shot eyes, and sporting silver earrings. There were two men from Beaucaire, a baker and his dough mixer, ruddy and wheezy, as befits their trade, but with the magnificent profiles of a roman Emperor. Lastly there was this fellow; no, not a person, really, just a cap. You were only aware of the cap … an enormous rabbit-skin cap. He said little, gazing miserably at the passing road.

These characters, well known to each other, were speaking very loudly, and even more freely, about their personal business. The Ranger announced that he was making for Nîmes in response to a Magistrate's summons for pitch-forking a shepherd. They're hot-blooded, these Camargue folk. As for the men from Beaucaire; they were at each others throats about the Virgin Mary. It appears that the baker was from a parish dedicated to the Madonna, known in Provence as the Holy Mother, and always pictured carrying the baby Jesus in her arms. His dough-mixer, on the other hand, was a lay-reader at a new church dedicated to the Immaculate Conception, whose icon showed her with open arms and illuminated hands. The way they treated each other and their respective Madonnas, had to be seen to be believed:

—She's no more than a pretty girl, your "immaculate" lady!

—Well, you know what you can do with your Holy Mother!

—She was no better around Palestine than she should have been, yours!

—What about yours, the little minx! Who knows what she got up to. Only St. Joseph can answer that.

You'd have thought we were on the docks in Naples. In truth, it only needed the glint of a knife blade, I'm sure, to settle this fine theological point once and for all; that is if the driver hadn't intervened.

—Give us some peace. You and your Madonnas! he said laughingly, trying to make light of the Beaucairian dispute: it's women's stuff, this, men shouldn't get involved.

He cracked his whip, from his high perch, as if to emphasise to his lack of religious conviction and to bring the others into line.

End of discussion. But the baker, having been stopped in full flow, wanted to continue in the same vein, and turned his attention towards the miserable cap, still morosely huddled in its corner, and quietly sneered:

—You there, grinder, what about your wife? What side of the parish border does she stand on?

It was as though it was meant to be a joke; the whole cart-load of them erupted into uproarious laughter ... except the grinder himself, who didn't react to the remark. This prompted the baker to turn towards me:

—You don't happen to know his wife do you, monsieur? Just as well; she's a real queer fish; there can't be another one like her in Beaucaire.

The increasing laughter left the grinder unmoved except for a whisper, his eyes still downcast:

—Hush, baker.

But there was no stopping this interfering baker, and he warmed to his theme:

—He's an idiot! No man of the world would complain about having wife like that. There's never a dull moment when she's around! Think about it! A really gorgeous girl, who every six months or so, ups sticks and runs away, and, believe me, always has a pretty tale to tell when she gets back ... that's the way it is ... a funny old menagerie, that one. Work it out, monsieur, they hadn't even been hitched a year when she breezed off to Spain with a chocolate merchant.

—The husband was inconsolable after that, sitting alone and drinking and crying all the time like a man possessed. After a while, she drifted back into the area, dressed like a Spaniard, complete with tambourine. We all warned her:

—You'd better get lost, he'll kill you.

—Kill her indeed ... Oh yes, I should say so, they made it up beautifully, she even taught him how to play the tambourine like a Basque!

Once again the coach rocked with laughter. Once again, the grinder still didn't budge, just murmured again:

—Hush, baker.

The baker ignored this plea and went on:

—You might think, after her return from Spain, monsieur, the little beauty would keep herself to herself?. But oh no!... Her husband accepted the situation again, so easily, it has to be said, that she was at it again. After Spain, there was an army officer, then a sailor from the Rhone, then a musician, then ... who knows?... What is certain, is that, every time, it's the same French farce ... She leaves, he cries; she comes back, he gets over it. You'd better believe it, he's a long suffering cuckold that one. But you've got to admit, she is a real good-looker, the little she-grinder; a piece fit for a king, full of life, sweet as could be, and a lovely bit of stuff. To top it all, she has a skin like alabaster and hazel eyes that always seem to be smiling at men. My word, Paris, if you ever pass through Beaucaire again....

—Oh do be quiet baker, I beg you..., the poor grinder went once again, his voice beginning to break up.

Just then the diligence stopped at the Anglores farm. Here it was that the two Beaucaire men got off, and believe me, I didn't try to stop them. What a trouble-maker sort of baker he was; even when he was in the farmyard, we could still hear him laughing.

With those two characters gone, the coach seemed empty. We'd dropped the Camargue Ranger in Arles and the driver led the horses on foot from there. Just the grinder and myself were left on top, each silent and alone. It was very warm; the coach's leather hood was too hot to touch. At times I could feel my head and eyelids getting heavy and tired, but the unsettling yet placid plea of "Be quiet, I beg you." kept echoing in my mind and wouldn't let me nod off. No rest for that poor soul either. I could see, from behind, that his broad shoulders were shaking, and his course, pale hand trembled on the back of the seat like an old man's. He was crying....

—This is your place, Paris! the driver said pointing out my green hillock with the tip of his whip, and there, like a huge butterfly on a hump, was my windmill.

I hurried to dismount ... but as I passed by the grinder, I wanted to get look at him under his cap before leaving. The unfortunate man jerked his head back as if reading my mind, and fixed me with his eyes:

—Mark me well, friend, he mumbled, and if one day, you hear of a tragedy in Beaucaire, you can say you know who did it.

He was a beaten, sad man with small, deep-set eyes; eyes that were filled with tears. But the voice; the voice was full of hatred. Hatred is the weak man's anger. If I were the she-grinder, I'd be very careful.

Master-Miller Cornille's Secret

Francet Mamaï, an aging fife player, who occasionally passes the evening hours drinking sweet wine with me, recently told me about a little drama which unfolded in the village near my windmill some twenty years ago. The fellow's tale was quite touching and I'll try to tell it to you as I heard it.

For a moment, think of yourself sitting next to a flagon of sweet-smelling wine, listening to the old fife player giving forth.

"Our land, my dear monsieur, hasn't always been the dead and alive place it is today. In the old days, it was a great milling centre, serving the farmers from many kilometres around, who brought their wheat here to be ground into flour. The village was surrounded by hills covered in windmills. On every side, above the pine trees, sails, turning in the mistral, filled the landscape, and an assortment of small, sack-laden donkeys trudged up and down the paths. Day after day it was really good to hear the crack of the whips, the snap of the sails, and the miller's men's prodding, "Gee-up".... On Sundays, we used to go up to the windmills in droves, and the millers thanked us with Muscat wine. The miller's wives looked as pretty as pictures with their lace shawls and gold crosses. I took my fife, of course, and we farandoled the night away. Those windmills, mark me, were the heart and soul of our world.

"Then, some Parisians came up with the unfortunate idea of establishing a new steam flour mill on the Tarascon Road. People soon began sending their wheat to the factory and the poor wind-millers started to lose their living. For a while they tried to fight back, but steam was the coming thing, and it eventually finished them off. One by one, they had to close down.... No more dear little donkeys; no more Muscat! and no more farandoling!... The millers' wives were selling their gold crosses to help make ends meet.... The mistral might just as well not have bothered for all the turning the windmills did.... Then, one day, the commune ordered the destruction of all the run-down windmills and the land was used to plant vines and olive trees.

"Even during of all this demolition, one windmill had prevailed and managed to keep going, and was still bravely turning on, right under the mill factors' noses. It was Master-Miller Cornille's mill; yes, this actual one we're chewing the fat in right now."

"Cornille was an old miller, who had lived and breathed flour for sixty years, and loved his milling above all other things. The opening of the factories had enraged him to distraction. For a whole week, he was stirring up the locals in the village, and screaming that the mill factories would poison the whole of Provence with their flour. "Don't have anything to do with them," he said, "Those thieves use steam, the devil's own wind, while I work with the very breath of God, the tramontana and the mistral." He was using all manner of fine words in praise of windmills. But nobody was listening.

"From then on, the raving old man just shut himself away in his windmill and lived alone like a caged animal. He didn't even want Vivette, his fifteen year old grand daughter, around. She only had her grandfather to depend on since the death of her parents, so the poor little thing had to earn her living from any farm needing help with the harvest, the silk-worms, or the olive picking. And yet, her grandfather still displayed all the signs of loving Vivette, and he would often walk in the midday sun to see her in the farm where she was working, and he would spend many hours watching her, and breaking his heart....

"People thought that the old miller was simply being miserly in sending Vivette away. In their opinion, it was utterly shameful to let his grand-daughter trail from farm to farm, running the risk that the supervisors would bully and abuse her and that she would suffer all the usual horrors of child labour. Cornille, who had once been respected, now roamed the streets like a gypsy; bare-footed, with a hole in his hat, and his breeches in shreds.... In fact, when he went to mass on Sundays, we, his own generation, were ashamed of him, and he sensed this to the point that he wouldn't come and sit in the front pews with us. He always sat by the font at the back of the church with the parish poor."

"There was something mysterious about Cornille's life. For some time, nobody in the village had brought him any wheat, and yet his windmill's sails kept on turning. In the evenings, the old miller could be seen on the pathways, driving his flour-sack laden mule along.

—Good evening, Master-Miller Cornille! the peasants called over to him; Everything alright, then?

—Oh yes, lads, the old fellow replied cheerily. Thank God, there's no shortage of work for me."

"If you asked him where the work was coming from, he would put a finger to his mouth and reply with great seriousness: "Keep it under your hat! It's for export." You could never get anything more than that out of him.

"You daren't even think about poking your nose inside the windmill. Even little Vivette wouldn't go in there.

"The door was always shut when you passed by, the huge sails were always turning, the old donkey was grazing on the mill's apron, and a starved-looking cat was sunning itself on the windowsill, and eying you viciously.

"All this gave it an air of mystery causing much gossip. Each person had his own version of Cornille's secret, but the general view was that there were more sacks of money than sacks of flour in the windmill.

"Eventually, though, everything was revealed. Listen to this:

"One day, playing my fife at the youngsters dance, I noticed that the eldest of my boys and little Vivette had fallen in love. Deep down, I was not sorry; after all, Cornille was a respected name in our village, and then again, it had pleased me to see this pretty little bundle of fluff, Vivette, skipping around the house. But, as our lovers had lots of opportunities to be alone together, I wanted to put the affair on a proper footing at once, for fear of accidents, so I went up to the windmill to have a few words with her grandfather.... But, oh, the old devil! You wouldn't credit the manner of his welcome! I couldn't get him to open the door. I told him through the keyhole that my intentions were good, and meanwhile, that damned starved-looking cat was spitting like anything above my head.

"The old man cut me short and told me, unfairly, to get back to my flute playing, and that if I was in such a hurry to marry off my boy, I'd be better going to look for one of the factory girls. You can imagine how much these words made my blood boil, but, wisely, I was able to control myself, and left the old fool to his grinding. I went back to tell the children of my disappointment. The poor lambs couldn't believe it; and they asked me if they could go to speak to him. I couldn't refuse, and in a flash, the lovers went. When they arrived, Cornille had just left. The door was double locked, but he had left his ladder outside. The children immediately went in through the window to see what was inside this famous windmill....

"Amazingly, the milling room was empty. Not a single sack; not one grain of wheat. Not the least trace of flour on the walls or in the cobwebs. There wasn't even the good warm scent of crushed wheat which permeates windmills. The grinding machinery was covered in dust, and the starving cat was asleep on it.

"The room below had just the same air of misery and neglect: a pitiful bed, a few rags, a piece of bread on a step of the stairs, and notably, in one corner, three or four burst sacks with rubble and chalk spilling out.

"So—that was Cornille's secret! It was this plaster that was being moved by road in the evenings. All this, just to save the reputation of the windmill, to make people believe that flour was still being milled there. Poor windmill. Poor Cornille! The millers had finished the last real work a long time ago. The sails turned on, but the millstone didn't.

"The children returned tearfully and told me what they had seen. It broke my heart to hear them. I ran round to the neighbours straight away, explaining things very briefly, and we all agreed at once on what to do, which was to carry all the wheat we could lay our hands on up to Cornille's windmill. No sooner said than done. The whole village met up on the way and we arrived with a procession of donkeys loaded up with wheat, but this time the real thing.

"The windmill was open to the world.... In front of the door, crying, head in hands, sat Cornille on a sack of plaster. He had only just come back and noticed, that while he was away, his home had been invaded and his pathetic secret exposed.

—Poor, poor me, he said. I might as well be dead ... the windmill has been shamed.

"Then sobbing bitter tears, he tried to say all sorts of consoling words to his windmill, as if it could hear him. Just then, the mules arrived on the apron and we all began to shout loudly as in the good old days of the millers:

—What ho there, in the windmill! What ho there, Monsieur Cornille!!

"And there they were, stacked together, sack upon sack of lovely golden grain, some spilling over onto the ground all around....

"Cornille, his eyes wide open, took some of the wheat into the palms of his old hands, crying and laughing at the same time:

—It's wheat! Dear Lord. Real wheat. Leave me to feast my eyes.

"Then, turning towards us, he said:

—I know why you've come back to me.... The mill factory owners are all thieves.

"We wanted to lift him shoulder high and take him triumphantly to the village:

—No, no my children, I must give my windmill something to go at first. Think about it, for so long, it's had nothing to grind!

"We all had tears in our eyes as we saw the old man scampering from sack to sack, and emptying them into the millstone and watching as the fine flour was ground out onto the floor.

"It's fair to say that from then on, we never let the old miller run short of work. Then, one morning Master-Miller Cornille died, and the sails of our last working windmill turned for the very last time. Once he had gone, no one took his place. What could we do, monsieur? Everything comes to an end in this world, and we have to accept that the time for windmills has gone, along with the days of the horse-drawn barges on the Rhone, local parliaments, and floral jackets."

Monsieur Seguin's Last Kid Goat

To Pierre Gringoire, lyrical poet, Paris.

You'll never get anywhere, Gringoire!

I can't believe it! A good newspaper in Paris offers you a job as a critic and you have the brass neck to turn it down. Look at yourself, old friend. Look at the holes in your doublet, your worn-out stockings, and your pinched face which betrays your hunger. Look where your passion for poetry has got you! See how much you have been valued for your ten years writing for the gods. What price pride, after all?

Take the job, you idiot, become a critic! You'll get good money, you'll have your reserved table in Brébant's, you will be seen at premieres, and it will secure your reputation....

No? You don't want to? You prefer to stay as free as the air to the end of your days. Very well then, listen to the story of Monsieur Seguin's last kid goat. You'll see where hankering after your freedom gets you.

Monsieur Seguin never had much luck with his goats.

He lost them all, one after another, in the same way. One fine morning they would break free from their tethers and scamper off up into the mountain, where they were gobbled up by the big bad wolf. Neither their master's care, nor the fear of the wolf, nor anything else could hold them back. They were, or so it seemed, goats who wanted freedom and open spaces whatever the cost.

Monsieur Seguin, who didn't understand his animals' ways, was dismayed. He said:

—It's all over. Goats get fed up here; I haven't managed to keep a single one of them.

But he hadn't totally lost heart, for even after losing six goats, he still bought a seventh. This time he made sure to get it very young, so she would settle down better.

Oh! Gringoire, she was really lovely, Monsieur Seguin's little kid goat; with her gentle eyes, her goatee beard, her black shiny hooves, her striped horns, and her long white fur, which made a fine greatcoat for her! It was nearly as delightful as Esmeralda's kid goat. Do you remember her, Gringoire? And then again, she was affectionate and docile, holding still while she was milked, never putting her foot in the bowl. A lovely, a dear little goat....

There was a hawthorn enclosure behind Monsieur Seguin's house where he placed his new boarder. He tied her to a stake in the finest part of the field, taking care that she had plenty of rope, and often went out to see how she was faring. The goat appeared to be very happy and was grazing heartily on the grass, which delighted Monsieur Seguin.

—At last, triumphed the poor man, this one isn't getting bored here!

Monsieur Seguin was wrong; his goat was becoming very bored.

One day, looking over towards the mountain, she remarked:

—How great it must be up there! How lovely to gambol on the heath without this rope tether that chafes my neck. It's alright for an ox or a donkey to graze all cooped up, but we goats should be able to roam free.

From then on, she found the grass in the enclosure bland. Boredom overcame her. She lost weight and her milk all but dried up. It was pitiful to see her pulling at her tether all day, with her head turned towards the mountain, nostrils flared, and bleating sadly.

Monsieur Seguin noticed that there was something wrong with her, but he couldn't work out what it was. One morning, as he finished milking her, she turned towards him and said to him, in her own way:

—Listen Monsieur Seguin. I am pining away here, let me go into the mountain.

—Oh my God. Not you as well! screamed Monsieur Seguin, dropping his bowl, stupefied. Then, sitting down in the grass beside his goat he added:

—So, my Blanquette, you want to leave me!

Blanquette replied:

—Yes, Monsieur Seguin.

—Are you short of grass here?

—Oh, no, Monsieur Seguin.

—Perhaps your tether is too short, shall I lengthen it?

—It-s not worth your while, Monsieur Seguin.

—Well then, what do you need, what do you want?

-I want to go up into the mountain, Monsieur Seguin.

—But, my poor dear, don't you realise that there is a big bad wolf on the mountain? What will you do when he turns up.

—I will butt him, Monsieur Seguin.

—The big bad wolf doesn't give a fig for your horns. He's eaten many a kid goat with bigger horns than yours. Have you thought about poor old Renaude who was here only last year? She was really strong and wilful, she was; more like a billy-goat. She fought off the wolf all night. In the morning the wolf still ate her, though.

—Poor, poor Renaude! But that doesn't alter anything, Monsieur Seguin, let me go into the mountain.

—Goodness!…, he said; What am I to do with these goats of mine? Yet another one for the wolf's belly. Well, I'm not going to have it, I will save you despite yourself, you rascal, and to avoid the risk of your breaking loose, I am going to lock you in the cowshed and you will stay there.

Without further ado, Monsieur Seguin carried the goat into the pitch blackness of the cowshed and locked and bolted the door. Unfortunately, he had forgotten to shut the window, and he had hardly turned his back when she got free.

Are you laughing, Gringoire? Heavens! I'm quite sure you are on the goats' side, and not Monsieur Seguin's. We'll see if you manage to keep laughing.

There was general delight when the white goat arrived on the mountain. The old fir trees had never seen anything nearly so lovely. She was received like a queen. The chestnut trees bowed down to the ground to stroke her with the tips of their leaves. The brooms opened up the way for her and brushed against her as best they could. The whole mountainside celebrated her arrival.

So, Gringoire, imagine how happy our goat was! No more tether … no more stake … nothing to prevent her from going where she wanted and nibbling at anything she liked. Hereabouts, there was lots of grass; she was up to her horns in it, my friend. And what grass! Delicious, fine, feathery, and dense, so much better than that in the enclosure. And then there were the flowers!… Huge bluebells; purple, long-stemmed foxgloves; a whole forest full of wild blooms brimming over with heady sap.

The white goat, half-drunk, wallowed in it, and with her legs flailing in the air, rolled along the bank all over the place on the fallen leaves in amongst the chestnut trees. Then, quite suddenly, she jumped confidently onto her feet. Off she went, heedlessly going forward through the clumps of boxwood and brooms; she went everywhere; up hill, and down dale. You would have thought that there were loads of Monsieur Seguin's goats on the mountain.

Clearly, Blanquette was not frightened of anything. In one leap, she covered some large torrential streams, which burst over her in a soaking mist. Then, dripping wet, she stretched herself out on a flat rock and dried herself in the sun. Once, approaching the edge of a drop, a laburnum flower in her mouth, she noticed Monsieur Seguin's house and the enclosure far down on the plain. It made her laugh till the tears came.

—How small it all is! she said; how did I manage to put up with it?

Poor little thing, finding herself so high up, she believed herself to be on top of the world.

Overall, it was a jolly good day for Monsieur Seguin's kid goat. About midday, scampering all over the place, she chanced upon a herd of chamois munching on wild vines with some relish. Our little minx in a white dress was an absolute sensation. All these gentlemanly bucks made way for her so she could have the very best of the vines…. It even seemed—and this is for your ears only Gringoire—that one of the black coated young chamois caught Blanquette's eye. The two lovers got lost in the trees for an hour or two, and if you want to know what they said to one another, go and ask the babbling brooks who meander unseen in the moss.

Suddenly, the wind freshened; the mountain turned violet; and evening fell….

—Already!, said the little kid goat, and stopped in astonishment.

In the valley, the fields were shrouded in mist. Monsieur Seguin's enclosure was hidden in the fog, and nothing could be seen of the house except the roof and a faint trace of smoke. She heard the bells of a flock of sheep returning home and began to feel very melancholy. A returning falcon just missed her with his wings as he passed over. She winced…. Then there was a howl on the mountain.

Now, the silly nanny thought about the big bad wolf; having not once done it all day. At the same time, a horn sounded far away in the valley. It was Monsieur Seguin making one last effort.

The wolf howled again.

—Come home! Come home! cried the horn.

Blanquette wanted to; but then, she remembered the stake, and the rope, and the hedged enclosure; and she thought that now she couldn't possibly get used to all that lot again, and it was better to stay put.

The horn went silent….

She heard a noise in the leaves behind her. She turned round and there in the shade she saw two short, pricked-up ears and two shining eyes…. It was the big, bad wolf.

Huge and motionless, there he was, sitting on his hindquarters, looking at the little white goat and licking his chops. He knew full well that he would eventually eat her, so he was in no hurry, and as she turned away, he laughed maliciously:

—Ha! Ha! It's Monsieur Seguin's little kid goat! and he licked his chops once again with his red tongue.

Blanquette felt all was lost. It only took a moment's thought about the story of old Renaude, who became the wolf's meal after bravely fighting all night, to convince her that perhaps it would have been better to get it over with, and to let herself be eaten there and then. Afterwards, thinking better of it, she squared up to the big bad wolf, head down, horns ready, like the brave little kid goat of Monsieur Seguin that she was ... not that she expected to kill him—goats don't kill wolves—but just to see if she could last out as long as Renaude....

As the big bad wolf drew near, she with her little horns set to into the fray.

Oh! the brave little kid goat; how she went at it with such a great heart. A dozen times, I'll swear, Gringoire, she forced the wolf back to catch his breath. During these brief respites, she grabbed a blade or two of the grass that she loved so much; then, still munching, joined the battle again.... The whole night passed like this. Occasionally, Monsieur Seguin's kid goat looked up at the twinkling stars in the clear sky and said to herself:

—Oh dear, I hope I can last out till the morning....

One by one the stars faded away. Blanquette intensified her charges, while the wolf replied with his teeth. The pale daylight appeared gradually over the horizon. A cockerel crowed hoarsely from a farm below.

—At last! said the poor animal, who was only waiting for the morning to come so that she could die bravely, and she laid herself down on the ground, her beautiful white fur stained with blood.

It was then, at last, that the wolf fell on the little goat and devoured her.

Goodbye, Gringoire!

The story you have heard is not of my making. If you ever come to Provence, our tenant farmers often tell you, of M. Seguin's kid goat, who fought the big bad wolf all night before he ate her in the morning.

Think about it, Gringoire, the big bad wolf ate her in the morning.

The Stars

A tale from a Provencal shepherd.

When I used to be in charge of the animals on the Luberon, I was in the pasture for many weeks with my dog Labri and the flock without seeing another living soul. Occasionally the hermit from Mont-de-l'Ure would pass by looking for medicinal herbs, or I might see the blackened face of a chimney sweep from Piémont. But these were simple folk, silenced by the solitude, having lost the taste for chit-chat, and knowing nothing of what was going on down in the villages and towns. So, I was truly happy, when every fortnight I heard the bells on our farm's mule which brought my provisions, and I saw the bright little face of the farm boy, or the red hat of old aunty Norade appear over the hill. I asked them for news from the village, the baptisms, marriages, and so on. But what particularly interested me, was to know what was happening to my master's daughter, Mademoiselle Stephanette, the loveliest thing for fifty kilometres around. Without wishing to seem over-curious, I managed to find out if she was going to village fetes and evening farm gatherings, and if she still turned up with a new admirer every time. If someone asked me how that concerned a poor mountain shepherd, I would say that I was twenty years old and that Stephanette was the loveliest thing I had seen in my whole life.

One Sunday, however, the fortnight's supplies were very late arriving. In the morning, I had thought, "It's because of High Mass." Then about midday, a big storm got up, which made me think that bad road conditions had kept the mule from setting out. Then, just after three o'clock, as the sky cleared and the wet mountain glistened in the sunshine, I could hear the mule's bells above the sound of the dripping leaves and the raging streams. To me they were as welcome, happy, and lively as a peal of bells on Easter Day. But there was no little farm boy or old aunty Norade at the head. It was … you'll never guess … my heart's very own desire, friends! Stephanette in person, sitting comfortably between the wicker baskets, her lovely face flushed by the mountain air and the bracing storm.

Apparently, the young lad was ill and aunty Norade was on holiday at her childrens' place. Stephanette told me all this as she got off the mule, and explained that she was late because she had lost her way. But to see her there in her Sunday best, with her ribbon of flowers, her silk skirt and lace bodice; it looked more like she had just come from a dance, rather than trying to find her way through the bushes. Oh, the little darling! My eyes never tired of looking at her. I had never seen her so close before. Sometimes in winter, after the flocks had returned to the plain, and I was in the farm for supper in the evening, she would come into the dining room, always overdressed and rather proud, and rush across the room, virtually ignoring us.... But now, there she was, right in front of me, all to myself. Now wasn't that something to lose your head over?

Once she had taken the provisions out of the pannier, Stephanette began to take an interest in everything. Hitching up her lovely Sunday skirt, which otherwise might have got marked, she went into the compound, to look at the place where I slept. The straw crib with its lambskin cover, my long cape hanging on the wall, my shepherd's crook, and my catapult; all these things fascinated her.

—So, this is where you live, my little shepherd? How tedious it must be to be alone all the time. What do you do with yourself? What do you think about?

I wanted to say, "About you, my lady," and I wouldn't have been lying, but I was so greatly nonplussed that I couldn't find a single word by way of a reply. Obviously, she picked this up, and certainly she would now take some gentle malicious pleasure in turning the screw:

—What about your girlfriend, shepherd, doesn't she come up to see you sometimes? Of course, it would have to be the fairy Esterelle, who only runs at the top of the mountain, or the fabled, golden she-goat....

As she talked on, she seemed to me like the real fairy Esterelle. She threw her head back with a cheeky laugh and hurried away, which made her visit seem like a dream.

—Goodbye, shepherd.

—Bye, Bye, lady.

And there she was—gone—taking the empty baskets with her.

As she disappeared along the steep path, stones disturbed by the mule's hooves, seemed to take my heart with them as they rolled away. I could hear them for a very long time. For the rest of the day, I stood there daydreaming, hardly daring to move, fearing to break the spell. Towards the evening, as the base of the valleys became a deeper blue, and the bleating animals flocked together for their return to the compound, I heard someone calling to me on the way down, and there she was; mademoiselle herself. But she wasn't laughing any more; she was trembling, and wet, and fearful, and cold. She would have me believe that at the bottom of the hill, she had found the River Sorgue was swollen by the rain storm and, wanting to cross at all costs, had risked getting drowned. The worse thing, was that at that time of night, there was no chance of her getting back to the farm. She would never be able to find the way to the crossing place alone, and I couldn't leave the flock. The thought of staying the night on the mountain troubled her a great deal, particularly as her family would worry about her. I reassured her as best I could:

—The nights are short in July, my Lady. It's only going to seem like a passing, unpleasant moment.

I quickly lit a good fire to dry her feet and her dress soaked by the river. I then placed some milk and cheese in front of her, but the poor little thing couldn't turn her thoughts to either warming herself or eating. Seeing the huge tears welling up in her eyes, made me want to cry myself.

Meanwhile night had almost fallen. There was just the faintest trace of the sunset left on the mountains' crests. I wanted mademoiselle to go on into in the compound to rest and recover. I covered the fresh straw with a beautiful brand new skin, and I bid her good night. I was going to sit outside the door. As God is my witness, I never had an unclean thought, despite my burning desire for her. I had nothing but a great feeling of pride in considering that, there, in a corner of the compound, close up to the flock watching curiously over her sleeping form, my masters' daughter rested,—just like a sheep, though one whiter and much more precious than all the others,—trusting me to guard her. To me, never had the sky seemed darker, nor the stars brighter…. Suddenly, the wicker fence opened and the beautiful Stephanette appeared. She couldn't sleep; the animals were scrunching the hay as they moved, or bleating in their dreams. For now, she just wanted to come close to the fire. I threw my goat-skin over her shoulders, tickled the fire, and we sat there together not saying anything. If you know what's it's like to sleep under the stars at night, you'll know that, when we are normally asleep, a mysterious world awakens in the solitude and silence. It's the time the springs babble more clearly, and the ponds light up their will o' the wisps. All mountain spirits roam freely about, and there are rustlings in the air, imperceptible sounds, that might be branches thickening or grass growing. Day-time is for everyday living things; night-time is for strange, unknown things. If you're not used to it, it can terrify you…. So it was with mademoiselle, who was all of a shiver, and clung to me very tightly at the slightest noise. Once, a long gloomy cry, from the darkest of the ponds, rose and fell in intensity as it came towards us. At the same time, a shooting star flashed above our heads going in the same direction, as if the moan we had just heard was carrying a light.

—What's that? Stephanette asked me in a whisper.

—A soul entering heaven, my Lady; and I crossed myself.

She did the same, but stayed looking at the heavens in rapt awe. Then she said to me:

—Is it true then, that you shepherds are magicians?

—No, no, mademoiselle, but here we live closer to the stars, and we know more about what happens up there than people who live in the plains.

She kept looking at the stars, her head on her hands, wrapped in the sheepskin like a small heavenly shepherd:

—How many there are! How beautiful! I have never seen so many. Do you know their names, shepherd?

—Of course, lady. There you are! Just above our heads, that's the Milky Way. Further on you have the Great Bear. And so, he described to her in great detail, some of the magic of the star-filled panoply....

—One of the stars, which the shepherds name, Maguelonne, I said, chases Saturn and marries him every seven years.

—What, shepherd! Are there star marriages, then?

—Oh yes, my Lady.

I was trying to explain to her what these marriages were about, when I felt something cool and fine on my shoulder. It was her head, heavy with sleep, placed on me with just a delightful brush of her ribbons, lace, and dark tresses. She stayed just like that, unmoving, right until the stars faded in the coming daylight. As for me, I watched her sleeping, being somewhat troubled in my soul, but that clear night, which had only ever given me beautiful thoughts, had kept me in an innocent frame of mind. The stars all around us continued their stately, silent journey like a great docile flock in the sky. At times, I imagined that one of these stars, the finest one, the most brilliant, having lost its way, had come to settle, gently, on my shoulder, to sleep....

The Arlesienne

As you go down to the village from the windmill, the road passes a farm situated behind a large courtyard planted with tall Mediterranean nettle trees. It's a typical house of a Provencal tenant farmer with its red tiles, large brown façade, and haphazardly placed doors and windows. It has a weather-cock right on top of the loft, and a pulley to hoist hay, with a few tufts of old hay sticking out....

What was it about this particular house that struck me? Why did the closed gate freeze my blood? I don't know; but I do know that the house gave me the shivers. It was choked by an eerie silence. No dogs barked. Guinea fowl scattered silently. Nothing was heard from inside the grounds, not even the ubiquitous mule's bell.... Were it not for white curtains at the windows and smoke rising from the roof, the place could have been deserted.

Yesterday, around midday, I was walking back from the village, by the walls of the farm in the shade of the old nettle trees, when I saw some farm-hands quietly finishing loading a hay wain on the road in front of the farm. The gate had been left open and discovered a tall, white-haired, old man at the back of the yard, with his elbows on a large stone table, and his head in his hands. He was wearing an ill-fitting jacket and tattered trousers.... The sight of him stopped me in my tracks. One of the men whispered, almost inaudibly, to me:

—Sush. It's the Master. He's been like that since his son's death.

At that moment a woman and a small boy, both dressed in black and accompanied by fat and sun-tanned villagers, passed near us and went into the farm.

The man went on:

—... The lady and the youngest, Cadet, are coming back from the mass. Every day it's the same thing since the eldest killed himself. Oh, monsieur, what a tragedy. The father still goes round in his mourning weeds, nothing will stop him.... Gee-up!

The wagon lurched ready to go, but I still wanted to know more, so I asked the driver if I could sit with him, and it was up there in the hay, that I learned all about the tragic story of young Jan.

Jan was an admirable countryman of twenty, as well-behaved as a girl, well-built and open-hearted. He was very handsome and so caught the eye of lots of women, but he had eyes for only one—a petite girl from Arles, velvet and lace vision, whom he had once met in the town's main square. This wasn't well received at first in the farm. The girl was known as a flirt, and her parents weren't local people. But Jan wanted her, whatever the cost. He said:

—I will die if I don't have her. And so, it just had to be. The marriage was duly arranged to take place after the harvest.

One Sunday evening, the family were just finishing dinner in the courtyard. It was almost a wedding feast. The fiancée was not there, but her health and well-being were toasted throughout the meal.... A man appeared unexpectedly at the door, and stuttered a request to speak to Estève, the master of the house, alone. Estève got up and went out onto the road.

—Monsieur, the man said, you are about to marry your boy off to a woman who is a bitch, and has been my mistress for two years. I have proof of what I say; here are some of her letters!... Her parents know all about it and have promised her to me, but since your son took an interest in her, neither she nor they want anything to do with me.... And yet I would have thought that after what has happened, she couldn't in all conscience marry anyone else.

—I see, said Master Estève after scanning the letters; come in; have a glass of Muscat.

The man replied:

—Thanks, but I am too upset for company.

And he went away.

The father went back in, seemingly unaffected, and retook his place at the table where the meal was rounded off quite amiably.

That evening, Master Estève went out into the fields with his son. They stayed outside some time, and when they did return the mother was waiting up for them.

—Wife, said the farmer bringing their son to her, hug him, he's very unhappy....

Jan didn't mention the Arlesienne ever again. He still loved her though, only more so, now he knew that she was in the arms of someone else. The trouble was that he was too proud to say so, and that's what killed the poor boy. Sometimes, he would spend entire days alone, huddled in a corner, motionless. At other times, angry, he would set himself to work on the farm, and, on his own, get through the work of ten men. When evening came, he would set out for Arles, and walk expectantly until he saw the town's few steeples appearing in the sunset. Then he turned round and went home. He never went any closer than that.

The people in the farm didn't know what to do, seeing him always sad and lonely. They feared the worst. Once, during a meal, his mother, her eyes welling with tears, said to him:

—Alright, listen Jan, if you really want her, we will let you take her….

The father, blushing with shame, lowered his head….

Jan shook his head and left….

From that day onwards, Jan changed his ways, affecting cheerfulness all the time to reassure his parents. He was seen again at balls, cabarets, and branding fetes. At the celebrations at the Fonvieille fete, he actually led the farandole.

His father said: "He's got over it." His mother, however, still had her fears and kept an eye on her boy more than ever…. Jan slept in the same room as Cadet, close to the silkworms' building. The poor mother even made up her bed in the next room to theirs … explaining by saying that the silkworms would need attention during the night.

Then came the feast day of St. Eli, patron saint of farmers.

There were great celebrations in the farm…. There was plenty of Château-Neuf for everybody and the sweet wine flowed in rivers. Then there were crackers, and fireworks, and coloured lanterns all over the nettle trees. Long live St. Eli! They all danced the farandole until they dropped. Cadet scorched his new smock…. Even Jan looked content, and actually asked his mother for a dance. She cried with joy.

At midnight they all went to bed; everybody was tired out. But Jan himself didn't sleep. Cadet said later that he had been sobbing the whole night. Oh, I tell you, he was well smitten that one….

The next morning the mother heard someone running across her sons' bedroom. She felt a sort of presentiment:

—Jan, is that you?

Jan didn't reply, he was already on the stairs.

His mother got up at once:

—Jan, where are you going?

He went up into the loft, she followed him:

—In heavens name, son!

He shut and bolted the door:

—Jan, Jan, answer me. What are you doing?

Her old trembling hands felt for the latch…. A window opened; there was the sound of a body hitting the courtyard slabs. Then … an awful silence.

The poor lad had told himself: "I love her too much…. I want to end it all…." Oh, what pitiful things we are! It's all too much; even scorn can't kill love….

That morning, the village people wondered who could be howling like that, down there by Estève's farm.

It was the mother in the courtyard by the stone table which was covered with dew and with blood. She was wailing over her son's lifeless body, limp, in her arms.

The Pope's Mule

When Provencal people talked about an aggressive man with a grudge, they used to say, "Beware of that man!… he is like the Pope's mule, who saved up her kick for seven years."

I have long been trying to find out where the saying came from, and what this papal mule and the seven year kick was all about. Nobody, not even Francet Mamaï, my fife player, who knows the Provencal legends like the back of his hand, has been able to tell me. Francet, like me, thinks that it is from an old tale from Avignon, but he has not heard of it elsewhere.

—You'll find it in the Cicada's open library, the old piper told me with a snigger.

It seemed a good idea to me, and, the Cicada's library being right outside my door, I decided to shut myself in for a week.

It's a marvellous library, well stocked, and open twenty four hours a day to poets and it is served by those little cymbal-clashing librarians who make music for you all the time. I stayed in there for several delightful days, and after a week's searching—lying on my back—I came up with just what I was looking for: my own version of the mule with the famous seven year grudge. The story is charming and simple, and I will tell it to you as I read it yesterday from a manuscript, which had the lovely smell of dried lavender, and long strands of maiden hair fern for bookmarks.

If you hadn't seen Avignon in papal times, you'd seen nothing. For gaiety, life, vitality, and a succession of feasts, no town was its peer. From morning till night there were processions, pilgrimages, flower strewn streets, high-hung tapestries, cardinals' arriving on the Rhone, buntings, galleries with flags flying, papal soldiers chanting Latin in the squares, and brothers' rattling their collecting boxes. There were such noises coming from the tallest to the smallest dwelling, which crowded and buzzed all around the grand Papal Palace, like bees round a hive. There was the click-click of the lace-makers' machines, the to and fro of the shuttles weaving gold thread for the chasubles, the little hammer taps of the cruet engravers, the twanging harmonic scales of the string instrument makers, the sing-songs of the weavers, and above all that, the peal of the bells, and the ever-throbbing tambourines, down by the bridge. You see, here in Provence, when people are happy, they must dance and dance. And then; they must dance again. When the town streets proved too narrow for the farandole, the fifers and tambourine players were placed in the cooling breeze of the Rhone, Sur le pont d'Avignon, where, round the clock, l'on y dansait, l'on y dansait. Oh, such happy times; such a happy town. The halberds which have never killed anyone, the state prisons used only to cool the wine. Never any famine. Never any war…. That's how the Comtat Popes governed their people, and that's why their people missed them so much….

There was one pope called Boniface who was a particularly good old stick. Oh, how the tears flowed in Avignon when he died. He was such a loveable, such a pleasant prince. He would laugh along with you as he sat on his mule. And when you got near to him—were you a humble madder plant gatherer or a great town magistrate—he blessed you just as thoughtfully. Truly, a Pope from Yvetot, but a Provencal Yvetot, with something joyful in his laugh, a hint of marjoram in his biretta, and no sign of a lady love…. The only romantic delight ever known to the good father, was his vineyard—a small one that he had planted himself amongst the myrtles of Château-Neuf, a few kilometres from Avignon.

Every Sunday, after vespers, this decent man went to pay court to the vineyard. As he sat in fine sunshine, his mule close by, his cardinals sprawled out under the vines, he opened a bottle of vintage wine—a fine wine, the colour of rubies, which has been known ever since as Château-Neuf du Pape—which he liked to sip while looking fondly at his vineyard. Then, the bottle empty and the daylight fading, he went merrily back to town, his whole chapter in tow. As he passed over the pont d'Avignon, amongst the drums and farandoles, his mule, taking her cue from the music, began a jaunty little amble, while he himself beat the dance rhythm out with his biretta. This shocked his cardinals, but not so the people, who were delighted by it, and said, "What a good prince! What a great pope!"

After his Château-Neuf vineyard, the pope loved his mule more than anything else on earth. The old man was quite simply besotted with the creature. Every night before going to bed, he made sure that the stable was locked and that there was plenty for her to eat. Also, he never rose from the table without a large bowl of wine, à la française, made with sugar, herbs, and spices, and prepared under his own watchful eye. He then took it, personally, to the mule, ignoring the cardinals' reproaches. Certainly, the beast was well worth the trouble, for she was a handsome, red-dappled, black mule, sure footed, glossy coated, with a large full rump and proudly carrying her small, slim head fully got up in pompoms, knots, silver bells and ribbons. She also showed an honest eye, as sweet as an angel's, and her ever-twitching long ears gave her a child-like, innocent appearance. Everybody in Avignon loved her, and when she was trotting through the streets, they all looked approvingly at her and made a great fuss of her; for everybody knew that this was the best way to gain the pope's favour. In all innocence, she had led many a one to good fortune, the proof of which lay in the person of Tistet Védène and his wonderful venture.

This Tistet Védène was, in truth, a mischief-maker, to the point where his father Guy Védène, the renowned goldsmith, had to run him out of the house, because he refused to do anything and coaxed the apprentices away from their work. For six months, he was seen hanging around every low place in Avignon. He was mainly to be seen near the Papal house, though, because this ne'er-do-well had something in mind for the Pope's mule, and, as you will see, it was something malicious…. One day, as His Holiness was out with his mule under the ramparts, along came Tistet and accosted him, clasping his hands together in feigned admiration:

—Oh, my lord, most Holy Father, what a splendid mule you have there!… Let me feast my eyes on her…. Oh, my dear Pope, she's a real beauty. I'll warrant the German Emperor doesn't have one like her.

Then he stroked her, and spoke gently to her as if she were a young lady:

—Come here, my jewel, my treasure, my priceless pearl….

The kind Pope was truly moved and thought to himself:

—What a fine young boy!… And how kind he is to my mule.

And the result? The very next day, Tistet Védène exchanged his old yellow coat for a beautiful lace cassock, a purple silk cape, and buckled shoes ready for his entry into the Pope's choir school. An establishment which, previously, had only taken in sons of the nobility or cardinals' nephews. That's how intrigue was done. But Tistet didn't stop at that.

Once he was in the Pope's service, the monkey did exactly the same tricks he had mastered before. He was insolent to everybody, having neither time nor consideration for anyone but the mule, and was to be seen for ever in the palace courtyard with handfuls of oats or bundles of sainfoin, gently shaking the pink bunches, as he looked at the Holy Father's balcony, with a look as if to say,

"Who's this lovely food for, then?" So much so, indeed, that finally the good Pope, who was beginning to feel his age, decided to leave the care of looking after the stable and taking the mule her bowl of wine, à la française, to none other than Tistet Védène. This did not amuse the cardinals.

As for the mule; it didn't amuse her at all…. From now on, at the time for her wine, she would witness five or six clerics from the choir school, with their lace and capes, get in amongst her straw. Then, shortly afterwards, a fine warm smell of caramel and aromatic herbs filled the stable, and Tistet Védène appeared carefully carrying the bowl of wine à la française. But the mule's agony was only just beginning.

This scented wine, which she loved so much, and kept her warm, and made her walk on air, was bought to her, in her very own manger, where it was put right under her nose. And then, just as her flared nostrils were full of it—it was cruelly snatched away—and the beautiful rosy red liqueur disappeared down the throats of those clerical brats…. If only they had been satisfied with just stealing the wine from her, but there was more to come. They were like demons, these clerical nobodies; after they had drunk the wine, one pulled her ears, another her tail; and while Quiquet mounted her, Béluguet tried his biretta on her. But not one of these thugs realised that with one butt or kick in the kidneys, the brave animal could have sent them all to kingdom come, or beyond. But, she wouldn't! She was not the Pope's mule for nothing, the mule associated with benedictions and indulgences. They often did their worst; but she kept her temper under control. It was just Tistet Védène that she really hated. When she felt him behind her, her hoof would itch to give him what for. The villainous Tistet played some terrible tricks on her. And after a drink or two, he came up with some very cruel inventions.

One day he decided to drive her up the bell tower of the choir school; to the very pinnacle of the palace. This really happened—two hundred thousand Provencal folk will tell you they've seen it! Imagine the terror of the luckless mule, when, after being shoved blindly up a spiral staircase and climbing who knows how many steps, she found herself suddenly dazzled on a brilliantly lit platform from where she could see the whole of a fantastic Avignon far below her, the market stalls no bigger than hazel nuts, the Pope's soldiers in front of their barracks looking like red ants, and there on a silvery thread, a tiny, microscopic bridge where l'on y dansait, l'on y dansait. Oh, the poor beast! She really panicked. She cried out loud enough to rattle the palace windows.

—What's the matter, what's happening to her? cried the Pope rushing to his balcony.

Tistet Védène, already back down in the courtyard, was pretending to cry and pull out his hair,

—Oh, most Holy Father, it's … it's your mule…. My lord, how will it all end? Your mule has climbed up into the bell tower….

—All alone?

—Yes, most Holy Father, all alone…. Look, look at her, up there…. Can't you see the end her ears sticking up?… They look like a couple of swallows from here….

—God help us! said the Pope beside himself and looking up…. She must have gone mad! She's going to kill herself…. Come down, you fool!…

Well! there was nothing she would have liked better … but how? The stairs were not to be entertained, you could climb them alright, but coming down was a different story; there were a hundred different ways to break your legs…. The poor mule was very distressed, and wandered about the platform, her huge eyes spinning from vertigo, and contemplated Tistet Védène,

—Well, you swine, if I get out of this alive … tomorrow morning will bring you such a kicking!

The thought of revenge revitalised her; without it she couldn't possibly have held on. At last, somebody managed to bring her down, but it was quite a struggle needing ropes, a block and tackle, and a cradle. Imagine what a humiliation it was for a Pope's mule to find herself hanging from a great height, legs thrashing about like a fly caught in a web. Just about everyone in Avignon was there to witness it.

The unhappy creature could no longer sleep at nights. She imagined that she was still spinning round on the cradle, with the whole town below laughing at her. Then her mind turned to the despicable Tistet Védène and the really good kicking that she was going to give him the very next morning. Oh, what a hell of a kicking that was going to be! The dust would be seen flying from far away…. Now, while the stable was being prepared for her, what do you think our Tistet Védène was up to? He was sailing down the Rhone, if you please, singing on a papal galley on his way to the court at Naples, accompanying the troupe of young nobles who were sent there by the town to practice their diplomacy and good manners in Italy. Tistet was no nobleman, but the Pope insisted on rewarding him for his care of the mule, particularly for the part he had just played in her rescue.

So, it was the mule who was disappointed the next day.

—Oh, the swine, he has got wind of something! she thought shaking her bells furiously…; but that's alright, go away if you must, you mischief-maker, you will still get your kicking when you get back…. I will save it for you!

And save it for him, she did.

After Tistet's departure, the Pope's mule returned to her tranquil life and ways of the old times. No more Quiquet, or Béluguet in the stable. The happy days of wine à la française returned, and with them came contentment, long siestas, and even the chance to do her own little gavotte once again, when she went sur le pont d'Avignon. And yet, since her adventure, she felt a certain coolness towards her in the town. Whispers followed her on her way, old folks shook their heads, and youngsters laughed and pointed at the bell tower. Even the good Pope himself hadn't as much confidence in his furry friend and when he wanted a nap mounted on the mule, coming back from the vineyard on Sundays, he feared that he would wake up on top of the bell tower! The mule felt all this, but suffered it in silence, except when the name Tistet Védène was mentioned in front of her, when her ears would twitch and she would snort briefly as she whetted her iron shoes on the paving stones.

Seven years passed before Tistet Védène returned from the court at Naples. His time over there wasn't finished, but he had heard that the Pope's Head Mustard-Maker had suddenly died in Avignon, and he thought the position was a good one, so he rushed to join the line of applicants.

When the scheming Védène came into the palace, he had grown and broadened out so much, that the Holy Father hardly recognised him. It has to be admitted though that the Pope himself had aged and couldn't see too well without his spectacles.

Tistet wasn't one to be intimidated.

—Most Holy Father, can you not recognise me? It is I, Tistet Védène....

—Védène?...

—Yes, you know me well.... I once served the wine, à la française, to your mule.

—Oh, yes, yes.... I remember.... A good little boy, Tistet Védène.... And now, what can we do for him?

—Oh, not a lot, most Holy Father.... I came to ask you something.... By the way, have you still got your mule? Is she keeping well?... Oh, that's good.... I came to ask you for the position of your Head Mustard-Maker, who has just died.

—Head Mustard-Maker, you! You're far too young. How old are you, now?

—Twenty years and two months, great pontiff, exactly five years older than your mule.... Oh, what a prize of God, a fine beast! If you only knew how much I loved that mule and how much I longed for her in Italy. Please may I see her?

—Yes, my child, you may see her, said the good, and by now, very moved Pope, and, as you care so much for the dear thing, I don't want you to live too far away. From this day forward, I am appointing you into my presence in the office of Head Mustard-Maker.... My cardinals will protest, but so what; I'm quite used to that.... Come and see us tomorrow after vespers, we will give you the insignias of your office in the presence of our chapter, and then … I'll take you to see the mule and you can accompany us to the vineyard…. Well, well, let's do it….

I needn't tell you that Tistet Védène left the hall walking on air, and couldn't wait for the next day's ceremony. And yet, there was someone in the palace, someone even happier and more impatient than he. Yes, it was the mule. From the moment Védène returned, right until the next day's vespers, the fearsome beast never stopped stuffing herself with hay and kicking her rear hoofs out at the wall. She, too, was making her own special preparations for the ceremony….

And so, the next day, after vespers, Tistet Védène made his entry into the courtyard of the papal palace. All the head clergymen were there, the cardinals in red robes, the devil's advocate in black velvet, the convent's abbots in their petite mitres, the church wardens of Saint-Agrico, and the purple capes of the choir school. The rank and file clergy were also there, the papal guard in full dress uniform, the three brotherhoods of penitentiaries, the Mount Ventoux hermits with their wild looks, and the little clerk who followed them carrying his bell. Also there were the flagellant brothers, naked to the waist, the sacristans, sprouting judge's robes, and all and sundry, even the holy-water dispensers, and those that light, and those that extinguish, the candles…. Not one of them was missing…. It was a great ordination! Bells, fireworks, sunshine, music and, as always, the tambourine playing fanatics leading the dance, over there, sur le pont d'Avignon….

When Védène appeared in the midst of the assembly, his bearing and handsome appearance set off quite a murmur of approval. He was the magnificent type of a man from Provence, from fair-headed stock with curly hair and a small wispy beard which could have been made from the fine metal shavings fallen from his goldsmith father's chisel. Rumour has it that Queen Jeanne's fingers had occasionally toyed with that blond beard. The majesty of Védène had indeed a glorious aspect; he had the vain, distracted look of men who have been loved by queens. On that day, as a courtesy to his native country, he had exchanged his Neapolitan clothes for a pink, braided jacket in the Provencal style, and a huge plume from an ibis on the Camargue fluttered on his hood.

The moment he entered as the new Head Mustard-Maker, he gave a general, gentlemanly greeting and made his way towards the high steps, where the Pope was waiting to give him his insignias of office: the yellow boxwood spoon and the saffron uniform. The mule was at the bottom of the steps, harnessed and ready to go to the vineyard.

As he passed her, Tistet Védène gave a broad smile, and paused to give her two or three friendly pats on the back, making sure, out of the corner of his eye, that the pope was watching.... The mule steadied herself:

—There you are! Caught you, you swine! I have saved this up for you for seven long years!

And she let loose a mule-kick of really terrible proportions, so that the dust from it was seen from a long way away—a whirlwind of blond haze and a fluttering ibis's feather were all that was left of the unfortunate Tistet Védène!...

Mules' kicks are not normally of such lightning speed, but she was a papal mule; and consider this; she had held it back for seven long years. There was never a better demonstration of an ecclesiastical grudge.

The Lighthouse on the Sanguinaires

It was one of those nights when I just couldn't sleep. The mistral was raging and kept me awake till morning. Everything creaked on the windmill, the whistling sails swayed heavily like ship's tackle in the wind, tiles flew wildly off the roof. The closely packed pines covering the hillside swayed and rustled far away in the darkness. You could imagine yourself out at sea....

All this reminded me of the bad spell of insomnia I had three years ago, when I lived in the Sanguinaires lighthouse overlooking the entrance to the gulf of Ajaccio on the Corsican coast.

I had found a pleasant place there where I could muse in solitude.

Picture an island with a reddish cast and a wild appearance. There was a lighthouse on one headland and an old Genoese tower on the other, which housed an eagle while I was there. Down by the sea-shore there was a ruined lazaretto, overgrown with grass. Then there were ravines, low scrub, huge rocks, wild goats, and Corsican ponies trotting about, their manes flowing in the breeze. At the highest point, surrounded by a flurry of sea-birds, was the lighthouse, with its platform of white masonry, where the keepers paced to and fro. There was a green arched door, and a small cast-iron tower on top of which a great multifaceted lamp reflected the sun and gave light even in the daytime. Well, that's what I recalled of the Isle of the Sanguinaires, on that sleepless night as I listened to the roaring pines. It was on this enchanted island that I used to fulfil my need for the open air and solitude before I found my windmill.

What did I do with myself?

Very much what I do here, or perhaps even less. When the mistral or tramontana didn't blow too hard, I used to settle down between two rocks, down by the sea amongst the gulls, blackbirds, and swallows, and stayed there nearly all day in that state between stupor and despondency which comes from contemplating the sea. Have you ever experienced that sweet intoxication of the soul? You don't think; you don't even dream; your whole being escapes, flies away, expands outwards. You are one with the diving seagull, the light spray across the wave tops, the white smoke of the ship disappearing over the horizon, the tiny red sailed boat, here and there a pearl of water, a patch of mist, anything not yourself.... Oh, what delightful hours, half awake and day-dreaming, I have spent on my island....

On days when the wind was really up, and it was too rough to be on the sea shore, I shut myself in the yard of the lazaretto. It was a small melancholy place, fragrant with rosemary and wild absinth, nestling against part of the old wall, where I let myself be gently overcome by that trace of relaxation and melancholy, which drifts in with the sun into the little stone lodges, open all round like old tombs. Occasionally, a gate would swing open or something would move in the grass. Once, it was a goat which had come to graze and shelter from the wind. When it saw me, it stopped, dumfounded, and froze, all agog, horns skyward, looking at me with innocent eyes.

At about five o'clock, the lighthouse keepers' megaphone summoned me to dinner. I returned only slowly towards the lighthouse, taking a small pathway through the scrub which ran up a hilltop overlooking the sea. At every step I glanced backwards onto the immense expanse of water and light that seemed to increase as I went higher.

It was truly delightful at the top. I can still recall now the lovely oak-panelled dining room with large flagstones, the bouillabaisse steaming inside, and the door wide open to the white terrace; all lit up by the setting sun. The keepers were already there, waiting for me before settling themselves down to eat. There were three of them: a man from Marseilles and two Corsicans; they all looked alike—small, and bearded, with tanned, cracked faces, and the same goat-skin sailor's jacket. But they had completely different ways and temperaments.

You could immediately sense the difference in the two races by their conduct. The Marseillais, industrious and lively, always busy, always on the move, going round the island from morning till night, gardening, fishing, or collecting gulls' eggs. He would lie in wait in the scrub to catch a passing goat to milk. And there was always some garlic mayonnaise or bouillabaisse on the hob.

The Corsicans, however, did absolutely nothing over and above their duties. They regarded themselves as Civil Servants and spent whole days in the kitchen playing cards only pausing to perform the ritualistic relighting of their pipes or using scissors to cut up large wads of green tobacco in their palms.

Otherwise, all three, Marseillais and Corsicans, were good, simple, straight-forward folk, and were full of consideration for their visitor, although I must have seemed a very queer fish to them....

The thought of someone coming to stay in the lighthouse for pleasure, was beyond their grasp. These were men who found the days interminably long and were ecstatic when their turn came to go ashore. In the warm season, this great relief came every month. Ten days off after thirty days on; that was the rule. In the winter, though, in rough weather, no rules could be enforced. The wind blew strongly, the waves ran high, the Sanguinaires were shrouded in white sea spray, and they were cut off for two or three months at a time, sometimes in terrible conditions.

—I tell you what happened to me, monsieur,—old Bartoli told me one day, while we were eating,—it was five years ago, at this very table, one winter evening, just like this one. That night, there were just the two of us, me and a fellow keeper called Tchéco…. The others were ashore, or sick, or else on leave…. I can't remember, now…. We were finishing our dinners, quite contentedly…. Suddenly, my fellow keeper stopped eating, looked at me with strange eyes, and fell forward onto the table with outstretched arms. I went to him; I shook him; I called his name:

"—Hey Tché!… Hey Tché!…

"No response! He was dead!… You can't imagine how I felt! I stayed there, idiot-like and trembling, next to the body for more than an hour. Then suddenly, I remembered,—The Light!—I only just had time to climb up to light the lantern—it was already getting dark….

"What a night, monsieur! The sea and the wind, they just didn't sound like they usually do. All the time somebody seemed to be calling to me from down the stairway…. I became frenzied; my mouth dried. But you couldn't have made me go down there again…. Oh no! I was too scared of the dead body. However, in the small hours, some of my courage returned. I went down and carried my mate back to his bed, covered him over with a sheet, said a short prayer, and then ran to raise the alarm.

"Unfortunately, the sea was too heavy; I shouted as loudly as I could, again and again, but to no avail, nobody came…. So, I was alone in the lighthouse with poor Tchéco, and for God knows how long. I was hoping to be able to keep him close to me until the boat came, but after three days that became impossible…. What should I have done? Carried him outside? Buried him? The rock was too hard and there are murders of crows on the island. It was a shame to leave a Christian to them. And then I decided to take him down to one of the lodges in the lazaretto…. That sad duty lasted a whole afternoon and, yes, it took some courage…. Look here, Monsieur, even today, when I go down to that part of the island through an afternoon gale, I feel that the dead man is still there, on my shoulders…."

Poor old Bartoli! Sweat ran down his forehead just thinking about it.

And so, our meals passed in long conversations about the lighthouse, and the sea, with tales of shipwrecks, and Corsican bandits.... Then, as night fell, the keeper of the first watch lit his hand-lamp, took his pipe, flask, and a red-edged, thick volume of Plutarch, which was the sum total of the Sanguinaires' library, and went down out of sight. A moment later, there was a crash of chains, pulleys, and heavy weights as the clock was wound up.

While this was going on, I went to sit outside on the terrace. The sun, already well down, hurried its descent into the water, dragging the whole skyline with it. The wind freshened; the island turned violet. In the sky a big bird passed slowly near me; it was the eagle homing to the Genoese tower.... Gradually, a sea mist got up. Soon, nothing could be seen except a white ridge of sea-fog around the island. Suddenly, a great flood of light emerged above my head from the lighthouse. The clear ray left the island in complete darkness as it fell far out to sea, and I, too, was lost to sight in the night, under the great luminous sweeps which barely caught me as they passed.... But the wind was freshening again. Time to go indoors. I groped to close the huge door, I secured the iron bars, and then, still feeling my way, took the small cast-iron stairs, which trembled and rang under my feet, to the top of the lighthouse. Here, as you can imagine, there was plenty of light.

Picture a gigantic lamp with six rows of wicks with the inner facets of the lantern arranged around them, some with an enormous crystal glass lens, others opened onto a large fixed glass panel which protected the flame from the wind.... When I came in, I was completely dazzled, and the coppers, tins, white metal reflectors, rotating walls of convex crystal glass, with large blue-tinged circles, and all the flickering lights, gave me a touch of vertigo.

However, gradually my eyes got used to it, and I settled down at the foot of the lamp, beside the keeper who was reading his Plutarch—for fear of falling asleep....

Outside, all was dark and desperate. On the small turning balcony, a maddening gust of wind howled. The lighthouse creaked; the sea roared. Out on the point, the breakers on the shoals sounded like cannon shots.... At times, an invisible finger tapped at the panes; it was some bird of the night, drawn by the light, braining itself against the glass....

Inside the sparkling, hot lantern, nothing was heard except the crackling flame, the dripping oil, the chain unwinding and the monotonous intoning of the life of Demetrius of Phaleron....

At midnight, the keeper stood up, took a last peek at the wicks and we went below. We passed the keeper of the second watch, rubbing his eyes as he came up. We gave him the flask and the Petrarch. Then, before retiring, we briefly entered the locker-room below, which was full of chains, heavy weights, metal tanks, and rope. By the light of his small lamp, the keeper wrote in the large lighthouse log, always left open at the last entry:

Midnight. Heavy seas. Tempest. Ship at sea.

The Wreck of the Semillante

The other night the mistral took us off course to the Corsican coast, so to speak. Let's stay there, as it were, while I tell you of an horrific event, often talked about by the local fishermen during their evening get-togethers, the details of which came to me by chance.

About two or three years ago, I was out sailing on the Sardinian Sea with seven or eight customs' men. A tough trip for a landlubber! There hadn't been a single fair day in the whole of March. The wind relentlessly pursued us and the sea never, ever, let up.

One evening, as we were running before the storm, our boat found refuge in the opening to the Straits of Bonifacio, in the midst of an archipelago.... They were not a welcoming sight: huge bare rocks covered with birds, a few clumps of absinth, some lenticular scrub, and here and there pieces of rotting wood half buried in the silt. But, believe me, for a night's stay, these ominous rocks were a much better prospect than the half-covered deckhouse of our old boat, where the waves made themselves very much at home. In fact, we were pleased to see the islands.

The crew had lit a fire for the bouillabaisse, by the time we were all ashore. The Master hailed me and pointed out a small outcrop of white masonry almost lost in the fog at the far end of the island:

—Are you coming to the cemetery? he said.

—A cemetery, Master Lionetti! Where are we then?

—The Lavezzi Islands, monsieur. The six hundred souls from the Sémillante are buried here, at the very spot where their frigate foundered ten years ago.... Poor souls, they don't get many visitors; the least we can do is to go and say hello to them, while we're here....

—Of course, willingly, skipper.

The Sémillante's crew's last resting place was inexpressibly gloomy. I can still see its small low wall, it's iron gate, rusted and hard to open, its silent chapel, and hundreds of crosses overgrown by the grass. Not a single everlasting wreath, not one remembrance, nothing! Oh, the poor deserted dead; how cold they must be in their unwanted graves.

We stayed there briefly, kneeling down. The Master was praying loudly, while gulls, sole guardians of the cemetery, circled over our heads, their harsh melancholy cries counterpoint to the sea's lamentations.

The prayer finished, we plodded, sadly, back to the spot where the boat was moored. The sailors had not wasted any time; we were met by a great roaring fire in the shelter of a rock, with a hot-pot steaming. We all sat around, feet drying by the flames, and soon everyone had two slices of rye bread to dunk into a soup-filled terra cotta bowl on our knees. The meal was eaten in silence; after all, we were wet, and hungry, and near to the cemetery.... However, once the bowls were empty, we lit our pipes and started to speak about the Sémillante.

—Well, how did it happen? I asked the boat's Captain, who was looking thoughtfully into the flames, head in hands.

—How did it happen? Captain Lionetti repeated by way of a reply. Then he sighed,—Alas, monsieur, nobody alive can tell you. All we know is that the Sémillante, loaded with troops bound for the Crimea, had left Toulon in bad weather the previous night. Later, things changed for the worse; wind, rain, and enormous seas the like of which had never been seen before.... In the morning, the wind moderated, but the sea was still in a frenzy. On top of that, the devil's own fog descended—you couldn't see a light at four paces. Those fogs, monsieur, you can't believe how treacherous they can be.... But it didn't make any difference, I believe the Sémillante must have lost her rudder that morning, for there is no such thing as a risk-free fog, and the Captain should never have gone aground there. He was a tough and experienced seafarer, as we all know. He had commanded the naval station in Corsica for three years, and knew his coast hereabouts as well as I; and it's all I do know.

—At what time do you think the Sémillante foundered?

—It must have been at midday; yes, monsieur, right in the middle of the day. But, my word, when it comes to sea fogs, midday is no better than a pitch-black night.... A local customs' officer told me, that at about half past eleven that day, as he went outside to close his shutters, the wind got up again and a gust blew his cap off. At the risk of being carried away himself, he began to scramble after it along the shore—on his hands and knees. You must understand that customs' men are not well off, and a cap is an expensive item. It seems that our man raised his head for a second and noticed a big ship under bare poles, running before the wind blowing towards the Lavezzi Islands. This ship was coming fast, so fast that he hardly had time to get a good look at her. No doubt it was the Sémillante because half an hour later, the island shepherd heard something on these rocks.... But here's the very shepherd I'm talking about, monsieur; he will tell you himself.... Good day, Palombo, don't be frightened, come and warm yourself.

Letters from my Windmill

45

A hooded man, whom I had seen a moment ago hanging around our fire, came timidly towards us. I had thought he was one of the crew, not knowing that there was a shepherd on the island.

He was an old, leprous person, not quite all there, and affected by some awful disease or other which gave him obscenely thickened lips, horrible to look at. We took great trouble to tell him what it was all about. Then, scratching his diseased lip, the old man told us that, yes indeed, from inside his hut he had heard a fearful crash on the rocks at midday on that day. The island was completely flooded, so he couldn't go out-of-doors and it wasn't until the next day that he opened up to see the shore covered in debris and bodies washed up by the sea. Horrified, he ran to his boat to try to get some help from Bonifacio.

The shepherd was tired by all this talking, and sat down, and the Master took up the story:

—Yes, monsieur, this was the unfortunate old man that came to raise the alarm. He was almost insane with fear, and from that day on, his mind has been deranged. The truth is, the catastrophe was enough to do it…. Imagine six hundred bodies piled up haphazardly on the beach with splinters of wood and shreds of sail-cloth…. Poor Sémillante…. The sea had crushed everything to such tiny fragments, that the shepherd, Palombo, couldn't find enough good timber to make a fence round his hut…. As for the men, practically all of them were disfigured and hideously mutilated…. it was pitiful to see them all tangled up together. We found the captain in full dress uniform, and the chaplain with his stole round his neck. In one place, between two rocks, lay the ship's young apprentice, open-eyed…. He looked as though he was still alive—but he wasn't. It was fated; no one could have survived.

Here the Master broke off his tale:

—Hey, Nardi, he cried, the fire's going out.

Nardi threw two or three pieces of tarred planking onto the embers which spluttered and then blazed. Lionetti continued,

—The saddest thing about this story is this…. Three weeks before the disaster, a small corvette, similar to the Sémillante, on its way to the Crimea was also wrecked in the same way, almost at the same place. This time however, we managed to save the crew and twenty soldiers in transit who were on board…. These unfortunate soldiers, you see, were not able to go about their business. We took them to Bonifacio and they stayed with us at the port for two days…. Once they were thoroughly dried out and back on their feet, we bade them farewell and good luck, and they returned to

Toulon, where they later set sail once again for the Crimea…. It's not too difficult to guess which ship they sailed on! Yes, monsieur, it was the Sémillante…. We found all twenty of them amongst the dead, just where we are now…. I, myself, recovered a good looking Brigadier with fine whiskers, a fresh-faced man from Paris, whom I had put up at my house and who had made us laugh continuously with his tales…. To see him there was heart breaking. Oh, Holy Mother of God!…

With that, Lionetti, deeply moved, knocked out his pipe and tottered off to his cabin wishing me goodnight…. The sailors spoke quietly to each other for a while, then they put out their pipes one by one. Nothing more was said. The old shepherd went off, and I remained alone, to mull things over, sitting amongst the sleeping crew.

Still affected by the horrendous tale I had just heard, I tried to reconstruct in my mind the unfortunate lost ship and the story of the agonising event witnessed only by the gulls. A few details struck me and helped me to fill out all the twists and turns of the drama: the Captain in full dress uniform, the Chaplain's stole, the twenty soldiers in transit. I visualised the frigate leaving Toulon at night. As she left the port, the sea was up, the wind was terrible; but the Captain was a valiant and experienced sailor and everybody on board was relaxed.

A fog got up in the morning. A sense of unease began to spread. The whole crew were on deck. The Captain stayed on the quarter-deck. In the 'tween-decks where the soldiers were billeted, it was pitch black, and the air was hot. Some of the men were sea-sick. The ship pitched horribly, which made it impossible to stand up. They talked in groups, sitting on the floor, clutching the benches for dear life; they had to shout to be heard. Some of them started to feel afraid. Listen, shipwrecks are common around those parts; the soldiers were there themselves to prove it, and what they said was not at all reassuring. Especially the Brigadier, a Parisian, who was always making quips that made your flesh creep:

—A shipwreck! How hilarious, a shipwreck. We are about to leave for an icy bath, and then be taken to Captain Lionetti's place in Bonifacio, where blackbirds are on the menu.

The soldiers laughed….

Suddenly, there was a great creaking sound….

—What the hell's that? What's going on?

—We've just lost the rudder, said a thoroughly sea-drenched sailor who was running through the 'tween-decks.

—Have a good trip! cried the never-say-die Brigadier, but this time the remark caused no laughter.

There was chaos on deck, but everything was hidden by the fog. The sailors were all over the place, scared, and groping about…. No rudder! Changing course was impossible…. The Sémillante could only run before the wind…. It was at that moment that the customs' officer saw her; it was half past eleven. In front of the frigate, a sound like a cannon shot was heard…. The breakers! the breakers! It was all up, there was no hope, ship and men together were going straight onto a lee shore…. The Captain went down into his cabin…. After a short time he reappeared on the quarter-deck—in full dress uniform… He wanted to look right when he died.

In the 'tween-decks, the soldiers were anxiously exchanged glances without saying a word…. The sick were doing their best to get on their feet…. Even the Brigadier wasn't laughing any more…. It was then that the door opened and the Chaplain appeared on the threshold wearing his stole:

—Kneel down, my children!

Those who could obeyed, and in a resounding voice, the priest began the prayer for the dying.

Suddenly, there was a formidable impact, a cry, one cry consisting of many, an immense cry, their arms fully tensed, their hands all clasped together, their shocked faces looking at a vision of death as it passed before them like a stroke of lightning….

Mercy!…

That is how I spent the whole night, ten years after the event, reliving, and evoking the spirit of the ill-fated ship whose wreckage was all around me. Far away, in the straits, the storm was still raging on. The camp-fire's flame was blown flat by a gust of wind, and I could hear our boat bobbing listlessly about at the foot of the rocks, its mooring squealing.

The Customs' Men

The boat Emilie from Porto-Vecchio, on which I had made the mournful voyage to the Lavezzi Islands, was a small, old, half-decked, customs' vessel, with no shelter available from the wind, the waves, nor even the rain, save in a small, tar covered deckhouse, hardly big enough for a table and two bunks. It was unbelievable what the sailors had to put up with in bad weather. Their faces were streaming, and their soaked tunics steaming, as if in the wash. In the depths of winter, these unfortunate souls spent whole days like this, crouching on their drenched seats, shivering in the unhealthy wet and cold, even at nights. Obviously, a fire couldn't be lit on board, and it was often difficult to make the shore…. Well, not one of these men complained. I always saw the same calmness and good humour in them, even in the most severe weather. And yet, what a gloomy life these customs' mariners led.

They were months away from going home, tacking and reaching around those dangerous coasts. For nourishment they had to make do mainly with mouldy bread and wild onions; they never once tasted wine or meat; these were expensive items and they only earned five hundred francs a year. Yes, five hundred francs a year. But it didn't seem to bother them! Everybody there seemed somehow content. Aft of the deckhouse, there was a tub full of rain water for the crew to drink, and I recall that after the final gulp went down, every last one of them would finish off his mug with a satisfied, "Ah!…"; a comic yet endearing indication of all being well with him.

Palombo, a small, tanned, thick-set man from Bonifacio was the merriest, and the most well at ease of all of them. He was always singing, even in the very worst weather. When the seas were high, when the sky was overcast, dark, and hail filled, everyone was all agog, sniffing the air, their hands cupped over their ears, listening and watching out for the next squall. Even in this great silence of anxiety on board, the voice of Palombo would begin the refrain:

No, dear Sir,
It will cause a stir.
Wise Lisette will stay,
And never ever go away….

And the gust could blow, rattle the tackle, shake and flood the boat, still the customs' man's song continued, rocking like a seagull on the crests of the waves. Sometimes the wind's accompaniment was too loud, and the words were drowned, but between each breaking wave, in the cascade of draining water, the little ditty was heard once again:

Wise Lisette will stay,
And never ever go away

One day, when it was blowing and raining hard, I didn't hear him. This was so unusual, that I was moved to emerge through the boathouse hatch and shout:

—Hey! Palombo, you're not singing, then?

Palombo didn't reply. He was lying apparently motionless under his bench. I went up to him; his teeth were chattering and his whole body was trembling feverishly.

—He's got a pountoura, his comrades miserably informed me.

This was what they called a stitch in the side, pleurisy. I had never witnessed a more miserable sight. There was an overwhelming, leaden sky, the boat had water cascading everywhere, the luckless, fevered man was wrapped in an old rubber coat which glistened like a seal's skin. The cold, the wind, and the jolting of the waves, soon made his condition worse. He became delirious; something had to be done.

After doing all we could, and as evening was approaching, we put into a small, silent, lifeless port, only animated by circling seagulls. The beach was shut in by steep-sided, high rocks, impassable scrub and sombre, unseasonably green shrubs. Nearby, close to the sea there was a custom's post, housed in a small white building with grey shutters. It was given a rather sinister air, this official outpost, numbered like the cap on a uniform, by its position, in the middle of such a deserted spot. We took the ailing Palombo down to it, though it was a despairing sanctuary for a sick man. We found the custom's man eating by the fireside with his wife and children. Everybody had a gaunt and jaundiced look, and they were pop-eyed and feverish. The young mother, suckling a baby, shivered as she spoke to us.

—It's a terrible post, the Inspector barely whispered to me. We have to replace our Customs' men here every two years. The marsh fever eats them away....

Nevertheless, the main thing was to get hold of a doctor. There wasn't one this side of Sartène, many kilometres away. What could we do? Our mariners were done and could do no more, and it was too far to send one of the children. Then the woman, leaning outdoors, called:

—Cecco!...Cecco!

And in came a large, well-built chap, a typical specimen of a poacher or Corsican bandit, with his brown wool cap and his goatskin sailors jacket. I had already noticed him, as we disembarked; he was sitting in front of the door chewing his red pipe, with a rifle between his legs. He made off as we came near; I don't know why. Perhaps he thought we had gendarmes with us. When he entered, the Customs' woman blushed.

—He's my cousin, she told us. There's no danger that this one will get lost in the Corsican scrub.

Then, she whispered something to him, indicating the sick man. The man bent forward but said nothing. Then he left, whistled his dog, and was gone, leaping from rock to rock with his long legs, with the rifle on his shoulder.

The children, who seemed terrified by the Inspector, quickly scoffed down their dinner of chestnuts and white Corsican goat cheese. Then there was the inevitable water; never anything but water on the table. And yet, a sip of wine would have really done the children some good. Oh, what complete and utter misery! After a while, their mother saw them off to bed, while their father lit his lantern and went out to check the coast. We stayed by the fireside looking after the invalid, who was tossing and turning on his pallet, as if he was still at sea being buffeted by the waves. We warmed up some stones to put on his side to ease his pleurisy. Once or twice the hapless man recognised me as I approached his bed and put out his hand with great difficulty by way of thanks. His broad hand was as rough and hot as one of the bricks from the fire.

It was a miserable vigil! Outside, as night fell, the bad weather picked up again, and there was a crash, a rumble, and a great spurt of spray, as the battle between rocks and water broke out again. From time to time, the gusts from out at sea blew into the bay and enveloped the house. The flames suddenly flared and lit up the blank faces of the sailors around the fireplace. They had the calm expression of those who routinely experience wide open spaces and horizons. Occasionally, Palombo moaned gently, and their eyes would turn towards the wretched place where the poor man was dying, far from home, and beyond help. Only their breathing and sighing could be heard. This was the only reaction you would get out of these workmen of the sea who were just as patient and accepting of their own misfortune. No rebellions, no strikes. Only sighs. Just sighs. And yet, perhaps I'm kidding myself. One of them, on his way to putting wood on the fire, whispered almost apologetically to me:

—You see, monsieur, there can be much suffering in our line of work....

The Cucugnanian Priest

Every year, at the feast of the presentation of Jesus, the Provencal poets publish a wonderful little book overflowing with beautiful verse and great stories. I've only just received this year's copy, and inside I found this adorable little fable which I am going to try to translate for you, albeit in a slightly abridged version.... Men of Paris, prepare yourselves for a treat. The finest flowering of Provencal flour is to be laid before you, right now....

Father Martin was the Cucugnan priest.

He was as wholesome as fresh bread, as good as gold, and he had a paternal love for his Cucugnanians. For him Cucugnan would have been the nearest thing to paradise on earth, if only the people had given him a little more, shall we say, business. But, sadly, his confessional remained unused except as a larder for spiders. On Easter day, the hosts remained secure in their holy ciborium. It hurt the good priest to the very centre of his soul, and every day he prayed that he would live to see his missing flock back in the fold.

Well, as you will see, the good Lord was listening.

One Sunday after the Gospels, monsieur Martin took his place in the pulpit.

—Bretheren, he said, believe me, or believe me not, the other night, I found myself, yes me, a miserable sinner, at the very gates of paradise.

"I knocked. St. Peter himself opened the gates!

"—Well! It's you, my dear monsieur Martin, he began, which fine wind...? And what can I do for you?

"—Dear St. Peter, keeper of the key and the great book, if I may be so bold, could you tell me how many Cucugnanians are in heaven?

"—I can refuse you nothing, monsieur Martin. Sit down, we will look it up together.

"St. Peter then took up his thick book, opened it, and put on his spec's:

"—Now then, let's see: Cucugnan, you say. Cu...Cu...Cucugnan. Here we are. Cucugnan.... My dear monsieur Martin, the page is purest white. Not a soul.... There are no more Cucugnanians than there are fish bones in a turkey.

"—What! There's no one from Cucugnan here? No one? That's impossible!

Look again, more closely….

"—Nobody, Oh, holy man. Look for yourself, if you think I am joking.

"—My, oh my! Dear, oh dear! I stamped my feet, clenched my hands and cried,—Mercy me!—Then, St Peter continued:

"—Believe me, monsieur Martin, you mustn't take on so, you could easily have a stroke. After all, it's not your fault. You see, your Cucugnanians must, without fear of contradiction, be doing their spell in purgatory.

"—Oh! for charity's sake, great St. Peter, make it so that I can at least see them to give them solace.

"—Willingly, my friend…. Here, put on these sandals, quickly, for the rest of the way is none too smooth…. That's right…. Now, keep going straight on. Can you see a turning over there, at the far end? You will find a silver door completely covered with black crosses…. On the right hand side…. When you knock, it will be opened unto you…. Bye-bye! Be good and, above all, stay cheerful."

"And I kept on going … and kept on going. I was dead beat, and covered in goose flesh; there was nothing to take my mind off things. A small footpath, full of brambles, and shining rubies and hissing snakes, led me to the silver door.

"I knocked twice.

"—Who is it? asked a hoarse, deathly voice.

"—The priest of Cucugnan.

"—Of…?

"—Of Cucugnan.

"—Ah!… Come in.

"I entered. A great, beautiful angel, with wings as dark as the night, a robe as radiant as the day, and a diamond key hanging at his waist, was scratching something into a great book even thicker than St.Peter's….

"—Well, what do you want; do you have a question? said the angel.

"—Dear angel of the Lord, I would like to know, I am dying to know, in fact, if you have the Cucugnanians here?

"—The?…

"—The Cucugnanians, the people from Cucugnan…. I am their prior.

"—Ah! Abbot Martin, is it?

"—At your service, monsieur angel."

"—Cucugnan, you say….

"The angel then opened his great book and leafed through it, licking his finger to turn the page....

"—Cucugnan, he gave a long sigh.... Monsieur Martin, we have no one here in purgatory from Cucugnan.

"—Jesus, Mary, and Joseph! No one from Cucugnan! Oh, Good Lord! So, where, forgive me, in heaven's name, are they, then?

"—Well! holy man, they are in paradise. Where on earth did you expect them to be?

"—But I've just come from there.

"—You've come from there!... And?

"—And! They're not there!... Oh, dear Mother of God!

"—What can I do monsieur priest? If they're neither in paradise not purgatory, there is no half way house, they are....

"—Holy Cross of Jesus, son of David! No, no, no, can it be?... Could it be that the great St. Peter himself lied to me?... I never heard the cock crow. Oh, we are lost! How can I possibly go to heaven if my flock aren't there?

"—Listen, my poor monsieur Martin, as you want to be sure about all this, no matter what, and to see for yourself what you have to do to turn things round, take that footpath, and run along it, if you know how to run.... You will come across a large gate on the left. There, it will all be made clear to you. And by God himself!

"And the angel closed the door."

"It was a long pathway covered in red-hot embers. I staggered as if I had been drinking; I stumbled at every single step; I was covered in sweat, a drop on every single hair of my body, and I was gasping for something to drink.... But, thanks to the sandals St. Peter lent me, I didn't burn my feet.

"After stumbling and limping along for some time, I saw a door on the left.... No, it was more a gate, an enormous, yawning gate, like a huge oven door. What a fantastic sight, my children! No one asked my name, even there at the reception area. I went through the cavernous door in batches, my brothers, just like you sinners as you go to the cabaret on Sunday night.

"I was sweating profusely, and yet frozen to the spot, I was trembling fearfully. My hair stood on end. I smelt burning, roasting flesh, something like the smell that spread around Cucugnan when Eli, the marshal, burned the hoof of an old ass while shoeing it. I couldn't breathe in that foetid, burning air; I heard a frightful clamour. There was moaning, howling, cursing.

"—You there! Are you coming in, or are you staying outside? scorned a horned devil, prodding me with his fork.

"—Me? I'm not going in. I am a friend of Almighty God.

"—So, you're a friend of God…. Eh! You damned fool! What are you doing here?…

"—I have come…. Oh! don't bother me, I can hardly stand up…. I have come … I have come from a far away … to humbly ask … if … if, by any chance, you have someone here from Cucugnan….

"—Oh! God's teeth! you're playing the idiot, you; it's as though you didn't know that the whole of Cucugnan is here. Well, ugly crow, watch and you will see how things are here with your precious Cucugnanians…."

"And I saw, in the middle of a terrible, flaming vortex of flame:

"The lanky Coq-Galine—you all knew him, my brothers—Coq-Galine, who was regularly drunk, and so often knocked ten bells out of his poor Clairon.

"I saw Catarinet … that little vixen … with her nose in the air … who slept alone in the barn…. You remember that, you rascals!… But let's move on, I've said too much already.

"I saw Pascal Doigt-de-Poix, who made his olive oil—with monsieur Julien's olives!

"I saw Babet the gleaner, who, as she gleaned, grabbed handfuls from the stacks to make up her quota!

"I saw Master Grapasi, who oiled his wheelbarrow rather a lot, so as not to be heard!

"And Dauphine, who greatly overcharged for water from her wells.

"And le Tortillard, who, when he met me carrying the Good Lord, rushed away, with his biretta perched on his head and his pipe stuck in his mouth … as proud as Lucifer … as though he had come across a mangy dog.

"And Coulau with his Zette, and Jacques, and Pierre, and Toni…."

Much moved and ashen with fear, the congregation whimpered, while imagining their fathers, and their mothers and their grandmothers and their sisters, when hell's gates were opened….

—Your feelings don't deceive you, brothers, the good abbot continued, you sense that this can't go on. I am responsible for your souls, and I do want to save you from the abyss towards which you are rushing helter-skelter and head first.

"Tomorrow, at the latest, my task begins. And the work will not be in vain! This is how I am going to go about it. For it to come out well, everything must be done in an orderly way. We will proceed step by step, like at Jonquières when there's a dance.

"Tomorrow, Monday. I will give confession to the old men and women. Nothing much there.

"Tuesday. The children. I'll soon have done.

"Wednesday. The young men and women. That might take a long time.

"Thursday. The men. We'd better cut that short.

"Friday. The women. I will tell them, not to build up their parts!

"Saturday. The miller. A day mightn't be enough for him.

"And, if we've finished by Sunday, we'll have done very well.

"Look, my children, when wheat is ripe, it must be harvested, when the wine is drawn, it must be drunk. We've had enough of dirty washing, what matters now is to wash it, and to wash it well.

"May you all receive God's loving grace. Amen!"

He was as good as his word. The washing was duly done.

From that memorable Sunday, the sweet smell of Cucugnanian virtue was heady for many kilometres around.

And the good priest, Monsieur Martin, happy and full of joy, dreamt one night that he was followed by all his flock, as he ascended in a candle-lit, resplendent procession, clouded in fragrant incense, with choir boys chanting the Te Deum. They were all following the light to the City of God.

There you are; the story of the priest of Cucugnan, as I was told by the great colloquial writer Roumanille, who had it himself from some other good fellow.

The Old Folks

—A letter, Father Azan?

—Yes, monsieur…. It's from Paris.

The good Father Azan was so proud that it came from Paris. Not me though. A little bird told me that this unexpected early-morning letter, which had just fallen into my lap, was going to cost me the rest of the day. I was not wrong, as you will see.

I must ask you for a favour, friend. I want you to lock up your windmill for the day and go directly to Eyguières. Eyguières is a large market town a few kilometres from here—an easy walk. When you get there, ask for the convent of the orphans. The first house after the convent is a single storey house with grey shutters and a small back-garden. Don't knock, just go in—the door is always open—and shout at the top of your voice: "Hello, folks! I'm Maurice's friend." You will then see two very old folks, hold out their arms to you from the depths of their large armchairs. Give them a heartfelt hug from me as if they were your own. Then, you might like to talk to them. They will be very boring about me, though, and tell you a thousand and one tales—but do listen respectfully—no laughing. You won't laugh will you?… They are my grandparents and I am everything in the world to them, but they haven't seen me for ten long years. I can't help it. Paris keeps me busy; and they are so old, so that even if they tried to visit me they couldn't make it. Fortunately, you will be there for them, my dear miller, and when you embrace them they will feel almost as if I were there. I have often mentioned you by name, and our special friendship which….

To hell with that sort of friend! It was fine weather, but certainly not walking weather; too much sun and too much mistral, a typical Provencal day to be sure. By the time this damned letter arrived, I had already decided on my bolt-hole for the day. It was to be in the shelter of two rocks, and I was looking forward to basking like a lizard and soaking up the Provencal light as I listened to the pines singing. Oh well, there was nothing else for it, I grumbled as I locked up the windmill, and put the key under the cat-flap. Cane, pipe, and I was on my way.

I arrived at Eyguières at about two o'clock. The village was deserted; everybody was out in the fields. In the white dust-covered elms in the courtyard, the cicadas were singing their hearts out, just like they do in the Crau plain. An ass was sunning itself in the town hall square, and a flock of pigeons were in the church fountain, but there nobody to direct me to the orphanage. Luckily, I came across an old fairy squatting and spinning her thread in a corner of her doorway; I told her what I was looking for, and, so powerful was she, that as she raised her distaff, the Convent of the Orphans appeared, as if by magic, before me.... It was a big, black, bleak house, proudly boasting an old red sandstone cross with a short Latin inscription above its pointed door arch. I spotted a smaller house next door with grey shutters, and a back-garden.... I recognised it immediately and went in without knocking.

The long, cool, quiet entrance hall made a life-long impression on me; with its pink painted wall, and faded flowers and violins on the panelling. I saw a small garden shaking about in the wind beyond a light coloured awning. I seemed to have come to the home of some sort of antediluvian bailiff.... At the end of the corridor on the left, the ticking of a large clock could be heard through a half opened door, and the voice of a school-age child, reading each syllable carefully. Th ... en ... Saint ... I ... re ... naeus ... cri ... ed ... I ... am ... the ... wh ... eat ... of ... the ... Lord ... I ... mu ... st ... be ... gro ... und ... by ... the ... tee ... th ... of ... th ... ese ... a ... ni ... mals.... I went gently over to the door and looked in.

In the quiet, and half-light of the small room, there was an old man with flushed cheeks, and wrinkled to the end of his finger tips. He was fast asleep, slumped in an armchair, with his mouth open and his hands on his knees. At his feet was a very young girl dressed all in blue—a large cape and a small bonnet—the orphanage's uniform. She was reading the life of St. Irenaeus from a book larger than herself.... This wonderful reading had a soporific effect on the whole household; the old man sleeping in his armchair, the flies on the ceiling, and even the caged canaries in the window. The big clock was quietly grinding away. Nothing moved in the room, except from within a large band of white light, which fell from between the closed shutters, which was full of sparkling movement and microscopic waltzes.... In the midst of all this general stupor, the child continued her solemn reading: S ... oon ... two ... lions ... jum ... ped ... on ... him ... and ... de ... vour ... ed ... him.... Then I appeared.... The actual arrival of the lions in the room could not have caused more panic. It was a moment of pure theatre! The tot screamed, the book fell, the canaries and flies bestirred themselves, the clock chimed, and the old man sat up, startled. I was a little flustered myself, and froze at the doorsill, shouting as loud as I could:

—Hello, folks! I'm Maurice's friend.

Well! You should have seen the poor old soul come with open-arms to hug me, and shake my hand, and pace wildly round the room, going:

—My God! My God!…

His wrinkled face broke into deep creases of laughter. He flushed and stuttered:

—Oh, monsieur… Oh, monsieur!…

Then he went to the back of the room and called out for:

—Mamette!

A door opened; a mouse-like scurrying was heard in the passage … and there she stood, Mamette, as pretty as a picture in her shell-like bonnet, her nun-like habit, and her embroidered hanky, which she held in the respectful, old-fashioned way…. It was so touching; they looked completely alike. With his hair done up and yellow shells, he could have been another Mamette, except that the real one must have cried a lot in her life, as she was even more wrinkled than he. She, too, had a girl carer from the orphanage, a little nurse, dressed in a blue cape, who never left her side. To see these old folks, cared for by the orphans, was unimaginably moving.

Mamette began by addressing me rather too formerly, but the old fellow cut her off mid-stream:

—He's Maurice's friend….

The effect was immediate; she stood there, trembling, crying, and blushing even more than he was. That's old people for you! Only a drop of blood in their veins, but at the least emotion, it leaps to their faces….

—Quick, get a chair, said the old woman to her little companion.

—Open the blinds, cried the old man to his.

The couple took a hand each, and trotted me over to the window, which they opened wide to get a better look at me. Once they got back into their armchairs, I sat down between them on a folding stool, and with the little blues stationed behind us, the grand interrogation began:

—How is he? What is he doing with himself? Why doesn't he come? Is he settled in?…

And so on and so forth—for hours on end.

I was answering all their questions as best I could, filling in the details that I knew, shamelessly inventing those I didn't, without ever admitting that I hadn't noticed if his windows were well-fitting, or the colour of his bedroom wallpaper.

—The bedroom wallpaper!… It's blue, madame, pale blue, with a floral pattern on it….

—Really? went the old lady fondly, and added turning to her husband:

"He's such a fine boy!"

—Oh yes, he's such a fine boy! he echoed enthusiastically.

All the time I was speaking, they shook their heads at one another, and chuckled, and gave knowing winks and nods to each other, then the old fellow drew close to me:

—Speak louder!… She's a bit hard of hearing.

And she said:

—Speak up, please!… He can't hear very well.…

So, I raised my voice, which evinced a grateful smile, and as these smiles faded I could just make out a faint image of Maurice. I was overwhelmed to see it; a vague, veiled, yet evasive, vision, as if I had seen my friend himself smile back at me, but in the misty distance.

Suddenly, the old man sat up in his armchair:

—I'm wondering, Mamette, if perhaps he hasn't had any lunch.

Mamette, shocked, threw her hands in the air:

—Not eaten!… Good Lord!

I thought they were still on about Maurice, and I was about to reassure them that their dear grandson always ate before midday, but it turned out it was actually me they were concerned about. There was some consternation when I admitted that nothing had passed my lips:

—Quick, lay the table, little blues! Put it in the middle of the room, use the Sunday-best table cloth, and the decorated plates. And do please stop giggling so much and make haste.…

Certainly, they did hurry, and the dinner was soon served up—three broken plates later.

—There you are, a fine breakfast for you! said Mamette, urging me to the table; "You will be dining alone, though, the rest of us have already eaten this morning."

The poor old things! Whatever the hour, they would have always claimed they'd already eaten.

All Mamette would have had for a breakfast, was a little bit of milk, some dates, and a tartlet—and that had to keep herself and her canaries going for a least a week. And to think that it was I who finished off their supplies!… Also, what indignation there was around at the table! The little blues, propped up on their elbows whispered to each other. From inside their cage, the canaries seemed to be saying, "What sort of man would eat all our tartlet!"

In fact, I did finish it off—almost unconsciously—I was busy looking around the light and peaceful room, where the scent of antiques seemed to drift in the air.... There were two small beds in particular, that I couldn't take my eyes off. I pictured the beds, almost as small as two cots, early in the morning when they are hidden under their great fringed curtains. Three o'clock chimes; the time when all old people wake up:

—Are you asleep, Mamette?

—No, my dear.

—Isn't Maurice a fine boy?

—Oh, yes, a fine boy?

And I imagined a whole conversation in that vein, inspired by just looking at the old folks' two little beds, laying side by side....

Meanwhile, quite a drama was taking place in front of the wardrobe at the other side of the room. There was a jar of cherries in brandy in the top drawer—waiting for Maurice for ten years—and which they now wanted me to have. Despite Mamette's pleas, the old fellow had insisted on getting the cherries down himself, and stood on a chair to try to reach them, to his wife's great horror.... Picture the scene: the old man trembling and hoisting himself up, the little blues clinging to his chair, Mamette puffing and blowing behind him, her arms outstretched. I caught a light scent of bergamot wafting from the open wardrobe with its large piles of discoloured linen.... It was a charming sight.

At last, after much struggling, the much vaunted jar was fetched from the drawer together with a dented old silver tumbler, which belonged to Maurice as a child. It was filled to the brim for me; although it was Maurice who loved cherries so much! While serving me, the old chap spoke into my ear with the air of someone who knew about gourmet things:

—You are very lucky, to be able to have these!... My wife made them herself ... you are about to taste something very good.

Unfortunately, while making them she had forgotten to add any sugar. What do you expect, you get absent-minded when you get old? The cherries were truly awful, my poor Mamette.... But it didn't stop me from eating them to very the last one, without batting an eyelid.

The meal finished, I stood up ready to take my leave. They really would have liked me to stay longer to chat about their precious grandson, but the day was drawing to a close, I was a long way from home, and it was time to go.

The old man stood up with me:

—Mamette, my coat!... I want to accompany him to the square.

Naturally, Mamette was quietly worried that it was a bit too cold now for him to go out, but she didn't let on; except, as she was helping him into his Spanish smoking jacket with mother of pearl buttons, I heard the dear old soul gently saying:

—You won't be out too long, will you?

—Ah, ha! I don't know, you'll have to wait and see … he answered, a touch mischievously.

With that, they exchanged looks and laughed, and the little blues joined in, a mood caught even by the canaries—in their chirping way…. Between ourselves, I think they had all been a bit intoxicated by the smell of the cherries.

… Night fell as the grandfather and I went out. His little blue followed us at a distance to help him home, but he never noticed her, and he was proud fit to burst, to walk on my arm like a man. Mamette, beaming, saw it from her doorstep and nodded her head as she looked in a way that seemed to say: "Well, well, he's my very own, dear, little man!… and he still has some go in him."

Prose Ballads

When I opened my door this morning, I was surprised by a great carpet of hoar-frost around the windmill. Grass sparkled and crackled like shattered glass; the whole hillside tinkled and twinkled.... For a day, my beloved Provence was dressed up as a northern land. It was here, amongst these ice-fringed pines, and clumps of lavender in crystal bouquets, that I wrote both these Germanic-style fantasies, prompted by the white frost gleaming at me and great V's of storks from Heinrich Heine's land made their way in a clear sky to the Camargue screaming, "It's cold ... it's cold ... it's cold."

I
DEATH OF THE DAUPHIN

The little Dauphin is sick; the truth is he's dying.... In every church in the Kingdom, the blessèd Sacrament is displayed night and day, and huge candles burn all the time for the recovery of the royal Child. The roads around the old residence are miserable and silent, the clocks don't chime, and the coaches go at walking pace.... Around the palace, through the railings, the curious bourgeoisie are watching some gold-draped, potbellied Swiss who are talking, self-importantly, in the courtyards.

The whole castle is troubled.... Chamberlains, and major-domos, scurry up and down the marble stairways.... The galleries are filled with silk-clad pages, and courtesans flitting from group to group seeking some whisper of news.... On the grand stairs, the weeping ladies-in-waiting hold themselves respectfully, and delicately wipe their eyes with finely embroidered handkerchiefs.

In the orangery, there were numerous gatherings of enrobed doctors. They can be seen through the windows adjusting their long, black sleeves and carefully rearranging their wigs.... The Dauphin's governor and his equerry are pacing about in front of the door, awaiting the doctors' prognostications. Some kitchen boys walk past them, without bowing. The equerry swears like a trooper; while the governor recites some verses by Horace.... Meanwhile, a long, plaintive whinny was heard from down in the stables. It was the young Dauphin's chestnut, now forgotten by its grooms, calling mournfully over its empty manger.

And the King? Where is His Majesty the King?... The King is all alone in a room, at the far side of the castle.... Royal Highnesses don't like to be seen crying.... It is another thing altogether with the Queen.... Sitting by the bedside of the little Dauphin, her beautiful face is bathed in tears, as she sobs out loud, in front of everybody, just as any commoner would.

In his lace-covered sick-bed, the little Dauphin, whiter than the cushions he lies on, has his eyes closed and looks fast asleep. But he is not. The little Dauphin turns towards his mother and seeing her in tears, says:

—Madame, why are you crying? Do you really think that I am dying?

The queen tries to answer, but the sobbing chokes her words.

—Don't upset yourself, madame. You are forgetting that I am the Dauphin and Dauphins can't die just like that....

The Queen's sobs intensify and the little Dauphin begins to feel afraid.

—Hang on, he says, I don't want death to come and take me, and I know just how to stop him from getting to me.... Have forty very strong soldiers mount guard around my bed!... Have a hundred big cannons ready under our window, tapers lit and fuses primed, day and night! And it's hard luck death if he dares to come near me!...

To please the Royal child, the Queen gives the order. Soon, big cannons are heard rolling in the courtyard, and forty tall German mercenaries, halberds at the ready, come and position themselves around the bed chamber. The little Dauphin claps his hands when he sees the old soldiers and their grey moustaches. He recognises one of them and calls out:

—Lorrain! Lorrain!

The soldier steps forward towards the bed:

—I really do like you, my dear Lorrain.... Have you brought your big sword.... If death comes for me, you will be sure to kill him, won't you?

Lorrain replied:

—Yes, Sire....

And two big tears run slowly down his tanned cheeks.

Just then, the Chaplain comes towards the young Dauphin and whispers to him for some time, showing him a crucifix. The little Dauphin listens, and looks astounded, and then, suddenly stops him:

—I can understand what you are telling me, Monsieur priest, but couldn't my little friend, Beppo die in my place, for which service we could give him a lot of money?...

The Chaplain continues the whispering and the little Dauphin looks more and more astonished.

As soon as the Chaplain finishes, the little Dauphin gives a huge sigh and says:

—Everything you tell me is so sad, Monsieur Priest, but if there's one thing that consoles me, it's that up there amongst the stars in paradise, I will still be the Dauphin…. I am sure that the Good Lord is my cousin and won't forget to treat me according to my rank.

Then, turning towards his mother, he adds:

—Have my best clothes brought to me; my white ermine doublet and my velvet court shoes. I want to make myself nice for the angels and enter paradise dressed as a Dauphin should.

For a third time, the Chaplain leans towards the little Dauphin and whispers to him for some time…. In the middle of his discourse, the Royal child interrupts him angrily:

—Well then, he cries, it's completely pointless being the Dauphin!

The little Dauphin has heard enough, and he turns towards the wall sobbing bitterly.

II

THE SUB-PREFECT TAKES A DAY OFF.

The Sub-Prefect was on his rounds. He was being carried majestically in the official barouche, complete with coachman and lackey, to the Combe-aux-Fée's Regional selection meeting. The Sub-Prefect had put on his best embroidered clothes; his opera hat, his skin-tight silver striped breeches, and his dress-sword with mother of pearl handle for this important day…. He was looking ruefully down at his knees, on which lies a large, embossed-leather, briefcase.

The Sub-Prefect was thinking about the speech which he must soon give before the residents of Combe-aux-Fées:

—Gentlemen and constituents….

But he might just as well have twiddled with his blond whiskers and repeated it twenty times for all the good it did:

—Gentlemen and constituents…. But nothing more of the speech would come.

Nothing more of the speech would come…. It was getting really warm in the barouche!… Under the Midi sun, the road to Combe-aux-Fées shimmers until it fades into the distance…. The very air burns you … and, at the roadside, thousands of cicadas are calling to each other, from one white, dust-covered elm to another…. Suddenly, the Sub-Prefect started. Down at the foot of a hill, he noticed a small wood of green oaks which seemed to beckon him.

The small wood of green oaks which seemed to beckon him:

—Come over here, Sub-Prefect, you will find composing your speech much easier in the shade of my trees....

The Sub-Prefect was captivated; he jumped down from the barouche and told his men to wait there for him, as he was going to compose his speech over in the small wood of green oaks.

In the small wood of green oaks, there were birds, violets, and springs hidden in the delicate grass.... When the birds noticed the Sub-Prefect with his gorgeous breeches and his large, leather-embossed briefcase, they became alarmed and stop singing, the springs are scared and stop their babbling, and the violets hid themselves in the grass.... This whole world in miniature had never seen a Sub-Prefect before, and they quietly wondered who this dignitary was, walking around in silver breeches.

Meanwhile, the Sub-Prefect, delighted by the silence and the coolness of the wood, lifted his coat-tails, put his hat on the grass, and sat down in the moss at the foot of a young oak. He then put the large, leather-embossed briefcase on his knees, opened it, and took out a long sheet of official paper.

—He's an artist, said the warbler.

—No, said the bullfinch, he's not an artist; with his silver breeches, he's more of a prince.

—He's more of a prince, said the bullfinch.

—He's neither an artist nor a prince, interrupted an old nightingale, who had sang all season in the district's gardens.... I know what he is; he's a Sub-Prefect!

And the whole woodland came alive with the rumour:

—He's a Sub-Prefect! He's a Sub-Prefect!

—He's bald! remarked a crested lark.

The violets asked:

—Is he a bad man?

—Is he a bad man? asked the violets.

The old nightingale replied:

—Not at all! And with that reassurance, the birds started to sing again, the streams to flow, and the violets to perfume the air, just as though the gentleman wasn't there.... Ignoring all this pretty clamour, the Sub-Prefect invoked the spirit of the country fêtes, and, pencil at the ready, began to declaim in his ceremonial voice:

—Gentlemen and constituents....

—Gentlemen and constituents.... said the Sub-Prefect in his ceremonial voice....

A cackle of laughter broke his concentration; he turned round and saw a lone fat woodpecker, perched on his opera hat, looking at him and laughing. The Sub-Prefect shrugged his shoulders and readied himself to continue, but the woodpecker interrupted him again:

—What is the point?

—I beg your pardon! What is the point? said the Sub-Prefect, who was flushing all over, and shooing the cheeky animal away, he resumed even more pompously:

—Gentlemen and constituents....

—Gentlemen and constituents.... once again resumed the Sub-Prefect even more pompously.

Then, the little violets stretched their stems out towards him and kindly asked him:

—Sub-Prefect, can you smell our lovely perfume?

And the streams were making divine music for him from beneath the moss, and over his head in the branches, a band of warblers sang their finest songs; indeed, the whole wood conspired to stop him composing his speech.

As he composed his speech, the Sub-Prefect was intoxicated by the perfume, and delighted by the music. He tried again to resist the charm, but in vain, and became completely overcome. He propped himself up on the grass with his elbows, loosened his fine tails, and stammers, yet again, two or three times:

—Gentlemen and constituents.... Gentlemen and const.... Gent....

Finally, he sent his constituents to the devil, and the muse of the country fêtes could only cover her face.

Cover your face, O Muse of the country fêtes!... When, after an hour, his assistants, worried about their master, followed him into the wood, they saw something that made them recoil in horror.... The Sub-Prefect was lying on his stomach in the grass, all dishevelled like a Bohemian. He had taken off his tails;... and the Sub-Prefect was composing poetry, as he chewed ruminatively on a violet.

Bixiou's Wallet

One October morning, a few days before I left Paris, a man in shabby clothes turned up at my home—while I was having lunch.

He was bent over, muddied, and stooped and shivered on his long legs like a plucked wading bird. It was Bixiou. Yes, Parisians, your very own Bixiou, the ferociously charming Bixiou, the fanatical satirist who has so delighted you for fifteen years with his writings and caricatures.... Oh, poor man, and how painful to see him like that. Without the familiar grimace when he came in, I would not have recognised him.

His head was bent over to one side, and his cane was pushed into his mouth like a clarinet. The illustrious and gloomy jester then moved to the centre of the room and staggered against my table as he said despondently: "Have pity on a blind man!..."

It was such a good take-off that I couldn't stop myself laughing. The Arctic-cold response came immediately: "If you think I'm joking ... just look into my eyes."

He then turned two large, white, sightless eyes towards me: "I've gone blind, my dear, blind for life.... That's what comes from writing with vitriol. I have burned out the candle of my eyes out doing the damned job ... to the stub!" he added showing me his desiccated eyelids with no trace of an eyelash.

I was so overcome, I couldn't find anything to say. My silence troubled him:

"Are you working?"

—No, Bixiou, I'm having lunch. Would you like to join me?"

He didn't reply, but I could see clearly from his quivering nostrils that he was dying to say yes. I took his hand and sat him down beside me.

While I served him, the poor devil sniffed at the food and chuckled:

"Oh, it smells good, this. I'm really going to enjoy it; and it will be an age before I eat again! A sou's worth of bread every morning, as I traipse through the ministries, is all I get.... I tell you, I'm really badgering the ministries now—it's the only work I do—I am trying to get permission to run a tobacconist's shop.... What else can I do; I've got to eat. I can't draw; I can't write... Dictation?... But dictate what?... I haven't a clue, me; I can't think of a thing to write. My trade was to look at the lunacies of Paris and hold a mirror up to them; but I haven't got what it takes now.... Then I thought about a tobacconist's shop; not in the boulevards of course, I can't expect those kind of favours, being neither a show girl's mother, nor a field officer's widow. No. I'm just looking for a small shop in the provinces, somewhere far away, say a spot in the Vosges. I will sell a hell of a clay pipe, and console myself by wrapping tobacco in my contemporaries' writings.

"That's all I want. Not too much to ask, is it? But, do you know what, its hell on earth to get it… Yet, I shouldn't be short of patronage. I have soared high in my time. I used to dine with the Marshal, the prince, and ministers, all those people wanted me then because I amused them—or frightened them. Now, no one does. Oh, my eyes! my poor, poor eyes! I'm not welcome anywhere, now. It's unbearable being blind at meal times…. Do pass me the bread, please…. Oh, those thieves! They will make me pay through the nose for this damned tobacconist's shop. I've been wandering through all the ministries clutching my petition, for the last six months. I go in the morning at the time they light the stoves and take His Excellency's horse around the sanded courtyard, and I don't leave until night when they bring in the big lights and the kitchens begin to smell really good….

"All my life is spent sitting on the wooden chests in the antechambers. The ushers know who I am, as well—enough said. Inside the court they call me That kind man! So, to get them on my side, to amuse them, I practise my wit, or, in a corner of their blotters, I draw rough caricatures without taking the pen off the page…. See what I've come to after twenty years of outstanding success; look at just what an artist's life amounts to!… And to think there are forty thousand rascals in France who slobber over our work! To think that throughout Paris, every day, locomotives make steam to bring us loads of idiots thirsting for waffle and printed gossip!… Oh, what a world of fantasists. If only Bixiou's suffering could teach them a lesson."

With that, and without another word, he pushed his face towards the plate and began to scoff the food…. It was pitiful to look at. He was losing his bread, and his fork, and groping for his glass all the time…. Poor soul! He just hadn't had the time to get used to it all yet.

After a short time, he spoke again:

"Do you know what's even worse? It's not being able to read the damned newspapers. You have to be in the trade to understand that…. Sometimes at night, when I am coming home, I buy one just for the smell of the fresh, moist paper, and newsprint…. It's so good! But there's not a soul willing to read it to me! My wife could, but she doesn't want to. She makes out that there are indecent things in the news items. Ah-ha! these old mistresses, once they marry you, there's no one more prudish. That Madame Bixiou has turned herself into a right little bigot—but only as far as it suits her!... It was she who wanted to me rub my eyes in Salette water. And then there was the blessed bread, the pilgrimages, the Holy Child, the Chinese herbal remedies, and God knows what else.... We're up to our necks in good works. And yet, it would be a real kindness to read the papers to me.... But there you are, there's no chance, she simply doesn't want to.... If my daughter was still at home, she would; but since I became blind, I've sent her to the Notre-Dame-des-Arts, so there'd be one less mouth to feed....

"Now there's another one sent to test me! She's only had nine years on earth and already she's had every imaginable illness... And miserable! And ugly! Uglier than I am, if that's possible ... a real monster!... What do you expect? I have never known how to face up to my responsibilities....

"Well, what good company I turned out to be, boring you with my family business. And what's it all got to do with you?... Come on, give me a bit more brandy. I'd better be off. When I leave here, I am off to the public information service and the ushers are not famed for their sense of humour. They're all retired teachers."

I poured him some brandy. He sipped it and then seemed moved by something.... Suddenly, on a whim, I think, he got up, glass in hand, and briefly moved his blind, viper-like head around, with the amiable smile of someone about to speak, and then speaking in a strident voice, as if holding forth to a banquet for two hundred,

"To the arts! To literature! To the press!"

And there he stood, spouting a toast for fully ten minutes. It was the most wild, the most marvellous improvisation which his clown's brain could devise.

"Imagine a year's-end revue entitled Collection of Letters of 186*; about our literati, our gossip, our quarrels, all the idiocies of an eccentric world, a cesspool of ink, hell in miniature, where you cut your own throat, disembowel yourself, rob yourself, and outtalk the bourgeoisie about interest rates and money. Where they let you starve to death better than anywhere else; all our cowardice and woes; old baron T... of la Tombola going away with a tut-tut to the Tuileries with his begging bowl and his flowery clothes. Then there's the year's deaths, the burial announcements, the never changing funeral oration of the delegate: the Dearly missed! Poor dear! over some unlucky soul who was refused the means to bury himself; the suicides; and those gone insane. Imagine all that, told, itemised, and gesticulated by an orator of genius, and you will then have some idea of what Bixiou's improvisation was about."

The toast over, his glass empty, he asked me what the time was, and left in a wild mood, without so much as saying goodbye.... I don't know how Monsieur Duruy's ushers were affected by his visit that morning; but I do know that after that awful blind man had left, I have never felt so sad, so bad, in the whole of my life.

The very sight of ink sickened me, my pen horrified me, I wanted to distance myself from it all, to run away, to see trees, to feel something good, real.... Good God! The hatred, the venom, the unquenchable need to belittle it all, to befoul everything! Oh! That wretched man....

Then I furiously paced up and down in my room still hearing the giggling disgust he had shown for his daughter. Right then, I felt something under my feet, near where the blind man had been sitting. Bending down, I recognised his wallet, a thick, worn wallet, with split corners, which he always carried with him and laughingly called his pocket of venom.

This wallet, in our world, was as famous as Monsieur de Girardin's cartoons. Rumour has it that there are some awful things in it.... I was soon to discover the truth of it. The old over-stuffed wallet had burst open as it fell and the papers inside fell onto the carpet; I had to collect them one by one....

There was a package of letters written on decorated paper, all beginning, My dear Daddy, and signed, Céline Bixiou at the Children of Mary hospital.

There were old prescriptions for childhood ailments: croup, convulsions, scarlet fever and measles.... (the poor little girl hadn't missed out on a single one of them!)

Finally, there was a hidden envelope from which came a two or three curly, blond hairs, which might have come from the girl's bonnet. There was some writing on it in a large, unsteady hand; the handwriting of a blind man:

Céline's hair, cut the 13th May, the day she went to that hell.

That's all there was in Bixiou's wallet.

Let's face it, Parisians, you're all the same; disgust, irony, evil laughter at vicious jokes. And what does it all amount to?...

Céline's hair, cut on the 13th May.

The Man with the Golden Brain

To the Lady who wants pleasant stories.

I took your letter, madame, as an invitation to change my ways. I have been tempted to shade my little tales a touch too darkly, and I promised myself to give you something joyful, wildly joyful, today.

After all, what have I got to be sad about? Here I am living hundreds of kilometres from the fogs of Paris, on a radiantly beautiful hillside, in the land of the tambourine and Muscat wine. Around my windmill, everything is sunshine and music; I have wind orchestras of wheatears, bands of blue-tits, and choirs of curlews from morning to midday. And the cicadas, and the shepherds playing their fifes, and the dark haired young beauties laughing amongst the vines…. To tell the truth, this is no place for brooding; I'd rather rush rose-coloured poems and basketsful of spicy stories to you ladies.

And yet—I can't. I am still too near to Paris. Every day, even here amongst my precious pines, it finds me with its ink-stained fingers of misery…. Even as I write, I have just heard the lamentable news of the death of poor Charles Barbara, and my windmill is plunged into grief.

Farewell, curlews and cicadas! I haven't the heart for jollity right now… For that reason, madam, instead of the pretty little tale which I had promised, you will only have yet another melancholy story today.

Once, there was a man with a golden brain; yes, madame, a brain made entirely from gold. At birth, the doctors thought he wouldn't survive long, so heavy was his head and so oversized his skull. However, he did live and he thrived in the sunshine like a lovely olive tree. Except that his huge head went everywhere with him and it was pitiful to see him bumping into all the furniture as he walked about the house….

All too often, he would fall down. One day, he fell from the top flight of some marble steps and just happened to catch his head on one. His head rang like an ingot. It could have killed him, but when he got up, there was nothing wrong except there was a small wound with two or three traces of congealed gold in his blond locks. That was how his parents learned that their child had a brain of pure gold.

It was kept a close secret, and the poor little thing himself suspected nothing. Sometimes he would ask why he wasn't allowed to go outside to play with the other boys in the street.

"Someone would steal from you, my treasure!" his mother told him.... Then the little lad, being terrified of being robbed, made no complaint as he went back to playing alone and dragging himself sadly from room to room....It wasn't until he was eighteen years old that his parents told him of this monstrous gift from fate. Since they had nurtured him and fed him all his life, they told him that it was about time he paid them back with some of his gold. The child didn't hesitate; he would do it that right then—but how?

The legend didn't tell him. He pulled out a nut sized piece of gold from his skull and placed it proudly onto his mother's lap.... Then, dazzled by the riches within his head, he became maddened by desire and drunk with power. So, he left the family home, and went out into the world to squander his treasure.

By the way he was living his life—royally—and spreading his gold around—lavishly—you would have thought his brain inexhaustible. And yet it did become exhausted—as could be seen by the dullness in his eyes and his pinched cheeks.

Finally, one morning, after a night of wild debauchery, the wretched boy, alone amongst the debris of the festivities and the dimming chandeliers, became terrified about the enormous hole appearing in his ingot of a brain. It was time to stop. From then on, he was like a new man. The man with the golden brain, went far away to live alone and work with his hands. He became suspicious and timid like a miser, turning his back on temptation, and trying to forget the fatal riches that he no longer wanted.... Unfortunately, a friend, who knew of his secret, had followed him. One night, the poor man was suddenly woken up by an excruciating pain in his head. He jumped up frantically and caught sight of the friend running away in the moonlight with something under his coat.... Another piece of brain had been stolen!...

Some time later, the man with the golden brain fell in love, and this time, too, it came out very badly....

He fell deeply in love with a petite, blond woman, who loved him a lot, too, but who loved fripperies, white feathers, and pretty, gold-tinged, tassels bobbling along the full length of her boots, even more. In the hands of this cute little creature—half bird, half doll—the gold pieces just melted away at her pleasure. She indulged every known whim, and he could never bring himself to say no to her. He even kept back the awful truth about his fortune to the very end, for fear of upsetting her.

—Are we really rich then? she would ask.

The poor man could only answer:

—Oh, yes... very rich!

And he would smile lovingly at the little blue bird who was unknowingly eating away at his head. Yet, sometimes fear took hold of him, and he had a craving to hang on to what little he'd got, but then the little woman bounded up to him and said:

—Husband, you are so rich! Buy me something really expensive....

And so, he brought her something really expensive.

Things continued like that for two years. Then, one morning, the young wife died, like a bird, no one knew why. Her funeral was paid for in gold, or at least with what was left of it. The widower arranged a lovely burial for his dear, departed wife. Peals of bells, substantial coaches done out in black, with plumed horses, and silver tears in the velvet drapery; nothing was too good for her. After all, what did the gold matter now?...

He gave some to the church, some to the pallbearers, and some to the everlasting-flower sellers. Oh yes, he spread it around alright, without stopping to count the cost.... By the time he left the cemetery, he had practically nothing left of his wonderful brain, only a few particles on the outside of his skull.

Then he was seen going out into the streets like someone lost, his hands stretched out in front of him, and stumbling like a drunkard. In the evening, as the shops lit up, he stopped in front of a large window with a well-lit, grand display of material and finery. He stood and glared for a long time at two blue satin bootees trimmed with swan down. "I know someone who will be very pleased with those bootees," he smiled to himself, and, in denial of his young wife's death, went straight in to buy them.

The shopkeeper, who was in the back, heard a great scream. She rushed out to help and jumped back in fear as she saw a man standing propped up against the counter and staring blankly at her. In one hand he had the blue bootees with swan down trimmings, and in the other was offering her some bloodied, gold scrapings in the end of his nails.

Such, madam, is the story of the man with the golden brain.

Despite it's air of fantasy, this story is true from start to finish.... Throughout the world there are unfortunate people who are condemned to live by their brains, and pay in that finest of gold, blood and sweat and tears, for the least thing in life. It brings them pain every day, and then, once they tire of their suffering....

The Poet, Frederic Mistral

Last Sunday, I thought I had woken up in Montmartre. It was raining, the sky was grey, and the windmill was a miserable place to be. I dreaded staying in on such a cold, rainy day, and I felt the urge to go and cheer myself up in the company of Frédéric Mistral, the great poet who lives a few kilometres from my precious pines, in the small village of Maillane.

No sooner said than gone; my myrtle walking stick, my book of Montaigne, a blanket, and off I went!

The fields were deserted…. Our beautiful catholic Provence gives the very earth itself a day of rest on Sundays…. The dogs are abandoned in the houses, and the farms are closed…. Here and there, was a carter's wagon with its dripping tarpaulin, an old hooded woman in a mantle like a dead leaf, mules dressed up for a gala, covered in blue and white esparto, red pompoms, and silver bells, jogging along with a cart-load of folks from the farm going to mass. Further on, there was a small boat on the irrigation canal with a fisherman casting his net from it….

There was no possibility of reading as I walked. The rain came down in bucketsful, which the tramontana then obligingly threw in your face…. I walked non-stop and after three hours I reached the small cypress woods which surround the district of Maillane and shelter it from the frightful wind.

Nothing was stirring in the village streets; everybody was at high mass. As I passed in front of the church, I heard a serpent playing, and I saw candles shining through the stained glass windows. The poet's home is on the far side of the village; it's the last house on the left, on the road to Saint-Remy—it's a small single-storey house with a front garden…. I went in quietly … and saw no one. The dining room door was shut, but I could hear someone walking about and speaking loudly behind it … a voice and a step that I knew only too well….

I paused in the whitewashed corridor, with my hand on the doorknob, and feeling very emotional. My heart was thumping.—He's in. He's working. Should I wait. Wait till he's finished…. What the hell. It can't be helped. I went in.

Well, Parisians, when the Maillane poet came over to show Paris his book, Mireille, and you saw him in your salons; this noble savage, but in town clothes, with a wing collar and top hat, which disturbed him and much as his reputation. Do you think that was Mistral? It wasn't.

There's only one real Mistral in the world, and that's the one that I surprised last Sunday in his village, with his felt beret, no waistcoat, a jacket, a red Catalonian sash round his waist, and fiery-eyed, with the flush of inspiration in his cheeks. He was superb, with a great smile, as elegant as a Greek shepherd, bestriding the room manfully, hands in pockets, and making poetry on the hoof....

—Well, well, well! It's you, Daudet? Mistral exclaimed, throwing himself around my neck, delighted that you thought to come!... Especially the day of the Maillane Fête. We've got music from Avignon, bulls, processions, and the farandole; it will be magnificent.... When mother comes back from the mass, we'll have lunch, and then, hey, we shall go to see the pretty girls dancing....

As he was speaking, I was rather moved as I looked around at the little dining room with light wallpaper, which I hadn't seen for such a long time and where I had spent such happy hours. Nothing had changed. There was still the yellow check sofa, the two wicker armchairs, Venus de Milo and Venus d'Arles on the fireplace, a portrait of the poet by Hébert, a photograph by Etienne Garjat, and his desk in a place close to the window—a small office desk—overloaded with old books and dictionaries. In the middle of the desk I noticed a large, open exercise book.... On it was written the original of his new poem, Calendal, which should be published on Christmas day this year. Frédéric Mistral has worked on this poem for seven years, and it is six months since he wrote the last verse, but he won't release it yet. You see, there is always another stanza to polish and another even more sonorous rhyme to find.... Even if Mistral writes his verses in true Provencal, he works as though everybody will read it and acknowledge his craftsmanship....

Ah, the brave poet. Montaigne must have had someone like Mistral in mind when he wrote, Think of those, who, when asked what is the point of spending so much time and trouble on a work of art that can only be seen by a few people, replied, "A few is enough. One is enough. None is enough."

The very exercise book in which Calendal had been written, was in my hands, and I leafed through it, with great emotion.... At that moment, fifes and tambourines began playing outside the window, and there was my hero, Mistral, rushing to the cupboard, fetching out glasses and bottles, and dragging the table to centre of the room, before opening the door to the musicians and confiding to me:

—Don't laugh…. They have come to give me a little concert…. I am a Municipal Councillor.

The little room filled up with people. Tambourines were put on chairs, the old banner placed in a corner, and the sweet wine passed round. After several bottles had been downed, to Monsieur Frédéric's health, the fête was seriously discussed, concerning such matters as whether the farandole was as good as last year, and if the bulls had played their part well. Then the musicians moved off to play concerts to other Councillors. Just then, Mistral's mother entered.

With a flick of her wrists, she laid the table with beautiful, white linen. But only for two. I was familiar with her household routine; I knew that when Mistral had company, his mother wouldn't sit down at the table…. The old dear only knows Provencal and would feel very uneasy trying to talk to French people…. Also, she was needed in the kitchen.

Goodness! I had a great meal that day—a piece of roast goat, some mountain cheese, jam, figs, and Muscat grapes. Everything washed down with a good Chateauneuf du Pape, which has such a wonderful red colour in the glass….

After the meal, I fetched the exercise book and put it on the table in front of Mistral.

—We'd said we'd go out, said the poet, smiling.

—Oh, no. Calendal! Calendal!

Mistral resigned himself to his fate and in his sweet musical voice, while beating the rhythm with his hand, he began the first canto:

Of a maid who fell in love and madly,
And a tale I told that turned out sadly,
Now of a child of Cassis,
If God's will it may be,
As a poor little boy casts out for anchovy…

Outside, the vesper bells ring, the fireworks explode in the square, and the fifes play marching up and down the streets with the tambourines. The bulls from the Camargue bellow as they are herded along.

But I was listening to the story of the little fisherman from Provence, with my elbows on the table cloth, and my eyes filling with tears.

Calendal wasn't just a fisherman; love had forged him into an heroic figure…. To win the heart of his beloved—the beautiful Estérelle—he took on Herculean tasks, in fact, those twelve famous labours paled by comparison to his.

One time, having it in mind to get rich, he invented some ingenious fishing devices to bring all the fish of the sea into port. Then there was this terrible bandit, count Sévéran, who was going to re-launch his evil trade amongst his cut-throats and molls....

What a tough guy our little Calendal turns out to be! One day, at Sainte-Baume, he came across two gangs of men intent on violently settling their hash on the grave of Master Jacques, a Provencal who did the carpentry in the Temple of Solomon, if you please. Calendal threw himself into the heart of the murderous mayhem, and calmed the men and talked them down....

These were superhuman efforts!... High up in the rocks of Lure, there was an inaccessible cedar forest, where even lumberjacks wouldn't go. Calendal, though, does go up there, all alone, and sets up camp for thirty days. The sound of his axe burying its head into tree trunks is heard the whole time. The forest screams its protest, but, one by one, the giant old trees fall and roll into the abyss, until, by the time Calendal comes down, there isn't a single cedar left on the mountain....

At last, in reward for so many exploits, the anchovy fisherman won the love of Estérelle and was made Consul of Cassis by its inhabitants. That's it then, the story of Calendal.... But why all this fuss about Calendal? The star of the poem is Provence itself—the Provence of the sea; the Provence of the mountains—with its history, its ways, its legends, its scenery, indeed a whole people, free and true to themselves, who have found their poetic voice, before they die.... Nowadays, follow the roads, the railways, the telegraph poles, hunt down the language in the schools! Provence will live for ever in Mireille and Calendal.

—That's enough poetry! said Mistral closing his notebook. To the fair!

We went out; the whole village was in the streets, as a great gust of wind cleared the sky, which radiantly lit up the red roofs, still wet with rain. We arrived in time to see the procession on its way back. It took a whole hour to go past. There was an endless line of hooded, white, blue, and grey penitents, sisterhoods of young, veiled girls; and gold flowered, pink banners, great faded, wooden saints carried shoulder high by four men. There was pottery saints coloured like idols with big bouquets in their hands, copes, monstrances, green velvet canopies, crucifixes framed in white silk; and everything waving in the wind, in the candle light and the sunlight, amongst the Psalms, the litanies, with the bells ringing a full peal.

Once the procession was over and the saints put back into their chapels, we went to see the bulls and then went on the open air games. There were men wrestling, the hop, skip and jump, and games of strangle the cat, and pig in the middle, and all the rest of the fun events of the Provencal fairs.... Night was falling by the time we got back to Maillane.

A huge bonfire had been lit in the square, in front of the café where Mistral and his friend Zidore were having a party that night… The farandole started up. Paper cut-out lanterns lit up everywhere in the shadows; the young people took their places; and soon, after a trill on the tambourines, a wild, boisterous, round dance started up around the fire. It was a dance that would last all through the night.

After supper, and too tired to keep going, we went into Mistral's modest peasant's bedroom, with two double beds. The walls are bare, and the ceiling beams are visible.... Four years ago, after the academy had given the author of Mireille a prize worth three thousand francs, Madame Mistral had an idea:

—Why don't we wallpaper your bedroom and put a ceiling in? she said to her son.

—Oh, no! replied Mistral…. That's poet's money that is, and not to be touched.

And so the bedroom stayed strictly bare; but as long as the poet's money lasted, anyone needy, knocking on Mistral's door, has always found his purse open….

I had brought the notebook with Calendal into the bedroom to read to myself a passage of it before going to sleep. Mistral chose the episode about the pottery. Here it is, in brief:

It is during a meal, somewhere or another. A magnificent Moustier's crockery service is brought out and placed onto the table. At the bottom of every plate, there is a Provencal scene, painted in blue on the enamel. The whole history of the land is represented on them. Each plate of this beautiful crockery has its own verse and the love in those descriptions just has to be seen. There are just so many simple but clever little poems, done with all the charm of the rural idylls of Theocritus.

Whilst Mistral spoke his verses in this beautiful Provencal tongue, more than three quarters Latin, and once spoken by queens, and now only understood by shepherds, I was admiring this man, and considering the ruinous state in which he found his mother tongue and what he had done with it. I was also imagining one of those old palaces of the Princes of Baux which can be seen in the Alpilles: there were no more roofs, no stepped balustrades, no glass in the windows; the trefoils broken in the ribbed vaults, and the coats of arms on the doors were eaten away and covered in moss. Chickens were scratching around in the main courtyard, pigs were wallowing under the fine columned galleries, an ass was grazing in the chapel overgrown with grass, and pigeons were drinking from the huge rain-water filled fonts. Finally, amongst the rubble, two or three peasant families had built huts for themselves against the walls of the old palace.

Then, one fine day, the son of one the peasants, develops a great passion for the grand ruins and is indignant to see them thus profaned. Quickly, he chases the livestock out of the courtyard and the muses come to help. He rebuilds the great staircase on his own, replaces the wood panelling on the walls, the glass in the windows, rebuilds the towers, re-gilds the throne room, and puts the one-time immense palace, where Popes and Emperors stayed, back on its pediments.

This restored palace: the Provencal language.

The peasant's son: Mistral.

The Three Low Masses

A Christmas Story.

I

—Two turkeys stuffed with truffles, Garrigou?...

—Yes, reverend, two magnificent turkeys, bursting out of their skins with truffles. I know something about it; it was I who helped to stuff them. It's fair to say that their skins are so tight, that a good roasting would split them....

—Jesus and Mary! I really do love truffles!... Give me my surplice quickly, Garrigou.... Is there anything else, apart from the turkeys, that you have noticed in the kitchen?...

—Oh! All sorts of good things.... We've done nothing but pluck birds since midday; pheasants, hoopoes, hazel grouse, and common grouse. Feathers flying everywhere. And from the lake; eels, golden carp, trout, and some ...

—How fat are the trout, Garrigou?

—As fat as your arm, reverend.... Enormous!...

—Oh, God! I think I've seen them.... Have you put wine in the cruets?

—Yes, reverend, I have put wine in the cruets.... But I assure you, it's nothing compared with what you will want to drink after you leave midnight mass. If you saw what was in the chateau's dining room, all the flaming carafes full of wine of all types.... And the silver dishes, the carved centre pieces, the flowers, the candelabras.... No one will ever have seen a Christmas dinner like this one. The Marquis has invited all the noble lords in the neighbourhood. There'll be at least forty at the sitting, not including the bailiff and the scrivener.... Oh, you are really lucky to be among their number, reverend!... There's nothing like sniffing these lovely turkeys, the smell of the truffles follows me around.... Mm....

—Come, come, my child, let us beware of the sin of gluttony, especially on Christmas Eve.... Hurry up, light the candles, and ring the first bell for mass, as midnight is upon us, and we mustn't be late....

This conversation took place one Christmas Eve in the year of our Lord sixteen hundred and God knows what, between the reverend Dom Balaguère, old prior of the Barnabites, then service chaplain of the Sires of Trinquelage, and his minor cleric Garrigou. At least he thought it was his minor cleric Garrigou, for, as you may know, that night the devil himself took on the round face and bland features of the young sacristan, in order to tempt the reverend father into the terrible sin of gluttony. So, as the so-called Garrigou was swinging his arms to ring the seigneurial chapel's bells, the reverend managed to put his chasuble back on in the small chateau sacristy, and with a spirit already troubled by gastronomic anticipation, he excited it even more as he dressed himself, by going over the menu,

—Roast turkeys ... golden carp ... trout as fat as your arm....

Outside the night-wind blew and broadcasted the music of the bells, as the lights began to appear on the dark side of Mount Ventoux, surmounted by the old towers of the Trinquelage. Tenant farmers' families were walking to hear midnight mass at the chateau. They sang as they climbed the hillside in small groups, the fathers in the lead, holding the lantern, their wives, wrapped up against the wind in large, brown mantles, which also acted as a shelter for the children when they snuggled up. Despite the dark and the cold, all these brave folk walked on joyfully, sustained by the thought that, just like every other year, after the mass, there would be a table stocked up for them in the kitchen downstairs. During the hard climb, a lord's coach, with its leading torch-bearers, and its windows shimmering in the moonlight, occasionally went by. Once, a mule with bells trotted past and the farmers were able to recognise their bailiff by the light of their lanterns, and greeted him as he passed:

—Good evening, Master Arnoton!

—Good evening, my dears!

The night was clear, the stars seemed intensified by the cold, and the wind was stinging. Very fine ice crystals slid down their clothes without wetting them, which kept up the tradition of a white Christmas. At the very top of the hill, the chateau marked the end of their journey, with its mass of towers and gables. The chapel's clock rose into a dark blue sky, and a host of tiny lights flickered in and out at every window in the murky rear of the building, and looked like sparks running along burning paper.... To reach the chapel, after crossing the drawbridge and passing through the rear entrance, you had to cross the main courtyard, full of coaches, valets, and sedan-chairs. It was all lit up by the fire of the torches and flares from the kitchens, which was also the source of a squeaking spit, clattering saucepans, the chink of crystal and silverware shaken about during the laying of the tables, and a warm steam smelling deliciously of roast meat and strong herbs in fine sauces. This started the farmers, chaplain, bailiff, and everybody else commenting:

—What a splendid Christmas Eve dinner there is in store for us!

II

The bell rings twice!…

Midnight mass is beginning. The candles are lit and the tapestries draped from top to bottom of the interleaved arches and the oak panelling in the chateau's chapel. It's a veritable cathedral in miniature. And what a congregation there is! And what get-ups they have on! The Sire of Trinquelage is dressed in salmon-pink taffeta in one of the choir's sculptured stalls, with all the other invited noble Lords sitting near him. Opposite, on a pair of velvet decorated prie-dieus, the old dowager marquise in her flame-red, brocaded dress, and the youthful Lady of Trinquelage, hair done up in a tower of crinkled lace in the latest style of the French court, have taken their places; and lower down, the bailiff, Thomas Arnoton, and the scrivener, Master Ambroy are all in black, and clean shaven, with huge pointed wigs—two quiet notes amongst the loud silks and brocaded damasks. Then the well-fed major-domos, the pages, the stablemen, the stewards, and Lady Barbe, with all her keys hanging by her side on a fine silver key-ring. Then comes the lower orders on benches; the servants, the tenant-farmers, and their families. Lastly, the male servers, who are lined up against the door, quietly half opening and closing it again, as they pop in and out between making sauces, so they can soak up a bit of the atmosphere of the mass. As they do this, a whiff of Christmas Eve dinner wafts into the middle of the service, already warmed by so many lit candles.

Is it the sight of these little white birettas which distracts the officiating priest? It's more likely to be Garrigou, with his persistent, little bell incessantly ringing on at the foot of the altar with infernal urgency as if to say:

—Hurry up, hurry up … the sooner we finish, the sooner we eat.

The simple fact is that with each tinkle of the devilishly insistent bell, the chaplain loses track of the mass, as his mind totally wanders off into the Christmas Eve banquet. He imagines the cooks buzzing around, the open-hearth blazing furnaces, the steam hissing from half-opened lids, and there, within the steam, two magnificent turkeys, stuffed to bursting, and marbled with truffles….

Even worse, he imagines the lines of pages carrying dishes that breathe out the tempting vapour and accompanies them to the great hall already prepared for the great feast. Oh, such delicacies! Then there is the immense table fully loaded and brimming over with peacocks still covered in their feathered glory, pheasants with their golden brown wings spread wide, the ruby coloured flagons of wine, pyramids of fruit begging to be plucked from the green foliage, and the marvellous fish spread out on a bed of fennel, their pearly scales shining as if just caught, with a bouquet of aromatic herbs in the gills of these monsters. So life-like is the vision of these marvels, that Dom Balaguère has the impression that these fabulous dishes were served on the embroidered altar cloth, so that instead of saying, the Lord be with you he finds himself saying grace. These slight faux-pas aside, he reels off his office conscientiously enough, without fluffing a line or missing a genuflexion. All went well to the end of the first mass. But, remember, the celebrant is obliged take three consecutive masses on Christmas Day.

—That's one less! sighs the chaplain to himself in blessèd relief. Then, without wasting a second, he nodded to his clerical assistant, or at least, to what he thought was his clerical assistant, and …

The bell rang, again!

The second mass begins, and with it, the fatal fall into sin of Dom Balaguère.

—Quick, quick, let's hurry up, cries the shrill voice of Garigou's bell, but this time the unlucky celebrant abandons himself utterly to the demon of greed and pounces on the missal, devouring the pages as he lost control of his avidly over-stimulated appetite. He becomes frenzied, he bows down, he rises, takes a sight stab at crossing himself and genuflecting, minimising the gestures, all the quicker to reach the end. His arms, no sooner stretched over the gospels than back thumping his chest for the I confess. Competition is joined between him and his cleric to see who finishes first in the mumbling stakes. Verses and responses tumble out and mix together. Half swallowed words through clenched teeth take too long, and so tail off into incomprehensible mutters.

—Pray for u …

—Thro … my fau …

Like frenzied grape-pickers treading the grapes from the vat, they squelched around in the Latin of the mass, slopping it all over the place.

—Lor … b'ith … yo… says Balaguère.

—An … wi … yo … spi't … replies Garrigou; and the busy little bell is more or less continuously in action jangling in their ears, acting like the bells they put on post-horses to make them gallop faster. To be sure, at this rate the second low mass is quickly dispatched.

—And the second one done! says the completely breathless chaplain. Then, without time for another breath, flushed and sweating, he rushes down the altar steps and….

The bell rings yet again!

The third mass is beginning. The dining room is no more than a few steps away, but, oh dear, as the Christmas Eve feast gets nearer, the unfortunate Balaguère is gripped by a mad, impatient fever of greed. His fantasies get the worse of him, he sees the golden carp, the roast turkeys, they are there, there right before his eyes…. He touches them … he … Oh God!… The steaming dishes, the scented wine; then the little bell frantically cries out,

—Faster, faster, faster!…

Yet how could he go any faster? As it was, his lips barely move. He doesn't even pronounce the words … short of completely fooling God and keeping His mass from Him. And then he even falls into that low state, the poor unfortunate man!… Going from bad to worse temptation, he begins to skip a verse, and then two. Then the epistle is too long, so he cuts it, skims over the gospel reading, looks in at the I believe but doesn't go in, jumps over the Our Father altogether, nods at the preface from afar, and goes towards eternal damnation by leaps and bounds. He was closely followed by the infamous, satanic Garrigou, who with his uncanny understanding as number two, lifts up his chasuble for him, turns the pages two at a time, bumps into the lecterns, knocks off birettas, and ceaselessly shakes the small bell harder and harder, faster and faster.

Those present are completely confused. Obliged to base their actions on the priest's words not one of which they understand, some stand up, while others kneel; sit down, while others stand. The Christmas star, yonder on its journey across the heavens towards the stable, pales in horror at the confusion which is happening….

—The father is going too quickly … we can't follow him, murmurs the old dowager as she distractedly plays with her hair.

Master Arnoton, his large steel-framed glasses on his nose, looks in his prayer book to see where on earth they might be in the service. At heart, none of these dear people, who are also thinking of the feast to come, are at all bothered that the mass is going at such a rate; and when Dom Balaguère, face beaming, turns towards the congregation shouting as loud as possible: The mass is over, it is as with one voice they make the response, so joyously and lively there in the chapel. You would think that they are already sitting at the table for the opening toast of the Christmas Eve feast.

III

Five minutes later, all lords, with the chaplain in the middle, are seated in the great hall. Everything is lit up in the chateau, which resounded with singing, shouting, laughter, and buzzing. The venerable Dom Balaguère is plunging his fork into a grouse wing and drowning his sinful remorse under a sea of wine and meat juices. The poor holy man eats and drinks so much that he dies in the night suffering a terrible heart attack, with no time to repent. So, the next morning, he arrives in a heaven full of rumours about the night's revelries, and I leave it for you to judge how he is received.

—Depart from me, you dismal Christian!, the sovereign judge, Our Lord, says to him. Your error is gross enough to wipe away a whole life of virtue.... Ah! You have stolen a midnight mass from Me.... Oh, yes you did! You will pay for your sin three hundred times over, in the proper place, and you will enter paradise only when you will have celebrated three hundred midnight masses, in your own chapel, in front of all those who have sinned with you, through your most grievous fault....

Well, that's that, the true story of Dom Balaguère as told in the land of the olive. The chateau of Trinquelage is no more, but the chapel still remains in a copse of green oaks at the top of Mount Ventoux. Now, it has a wind-blown, ramshackle door and grass grows over the threshold. There are birds' nests in the corner of the altar and in the window openings, from where the stained glass is long departed. However, it is said that every year at Christmas, a supernatural light moves amongst the ruins, and when the peasants go to the mass and Christmas Eve meals, they can see this ghostly chapel lit by invisible candles, which burn in the open air, even in a blizzard. Laugh if you will, but a winegrower in the area named Garrigue, no doubt a descendant of Garrigou, assures me that once, when he was a bit merry at Christmas, he got lost in the mountain around Trinquelage. This is what he saw....

Until eleven o'clock at night ... nothing. Everything was silent, dark, and still. Suddenly, towards midnight, a hand bell rang at the very top of the clock tower. It was an ancient bell which sounded as if it were coming from far away. Soon, Garrigue saw flickering lights making vague, restless shadows on the road. Under the chapel's porch, someone was walking and whispering:

—Good evening, Master Arnoton!

—Good evening, good evening, folks!...

When everyone had gone in, the winegrower, a very brave man, approached carefully, and, looking through the broken door, was met by a very strange sight, indeed. All the people whom he had seen pass were positioned around the choir in the ruined nave, as though the old benches were still there. There were beautiful women in brocade and lace-draped hair, lords in colourful finery from head to toe, and peasants in floral jackets like those our grandfathers used to wear. Everything gave the impression of being old, dusty, faded, and worn out. Sometimes, nocturnal birds, regular visitors to the chapel, attracted by the lights, came to flap around the candles whose flame went straight upwards but looked dim as if seen through gauze. There was a certain person in large, steel-framed glasses, who kept shaking his tall, black wig where one of the birds was completely entangled, its wings silently thrashing about, much to the amusement of Garrigue….

Deep inside, a little old man with a childish build, on his knees in the middle of the choir, was desperately and soundlessly shaking a clapper-less hand bell, while a priest in old, gold vestments was coming and going and toing and froing in front of the altar, and saying prayers, not a syllable of which could be heard. It was Dom Balaguère, of course, in the middle of his third low mass.

The Oranges

A FANTASY.

In Paris, oranges have the sorrowful look of windfalls gathered from beneath the trees. At the time they get to you, in the dreary middle of a rainy, cold winter, their brilliant skins, and their strong perfume—or so they seem to your Parisian mediocre tastes—imbue them with a foreign flavour, a hint of Bohemia. Throughout the foggy afternoons, they line the pavements, squashed together in wheelbarrows, lit by the low light of lanterns and wrapped in red paper. A thin, repetitive shout of:

—Valencian oranges, two sous a piece!

accompanies them, often drowned by the sound of cavorting carriages and boisterous buses.

For most Parisians, this fruit, gathered far away, and unremarkably round, with just a clipping of greenery from the tree, reminds them of sweets and desserts. The tissue they're wrapped in, and the parties at which they make their appearance, add to this impression. Come January, thousands of oranges are on the streets and their discarded skins are in the muddy gutters everywhere, looking as though some giant Christmas tree had shaken its branches of artificial fruit all over Paris. There's just about nowhere free of oranges; they are in the carefully arranged shop windows, sorted and prepared; outside prison and hospital gates, among the packets of biscuits and the stacks of apples, and in front of entrances to dances and Sunday street shows. Their exquisite perfume mixes variously with the smell of gas, the noise of old violins, and the dust in the gods at the theatre. It's easy to forget that it takes orange trees to make oranges, for when the fruit arrives from the Midi, by their thousands of boxfuls, the tree itself, pruned and unrecognisable, is hidden in a warm greenhouse for the winter and makes only a brief summer appearance in public gardens in Paris.

To really appreciate oranges, you have to see them in their natural setting; in the Balearics, Sardinia, Corsica, and Algeria; in the sunny blue skies of the warm Mediterranean. I can recall with great pleasure a small orchard of orange trees, at the gates of Blidah, just such a place where their true beauty could be seen! Amongst the dark, glossy, lustred leaves, the fruits had the brilliance of stained glass windows and perfumed the air all around with the same magnificent aura that usually envelops gorgeous flowers. Here and there, gaps in the branches revealed the ramparts of the little town, the minaret of a mosque, the dome of a marabout, and, towering above, the immense Atlas mountains, green at the base, and snow-capped, with drifts of snow here and there.

One night during my stay, a strange phenomenon, not seen for thirty years, occurred; the ice from the freezing zone descended onto the sleeping village, and Blidah woke up transformed, and powdered in white snow. In the light, pure Algerian air, the snow looked like the finest dusting of mother of pearl, and had the lustre of a white peacock's feather. But it was the orange orchard that was the most beautiful thing to be seen. The firm leaves kept the snow intact and upright like sorbets on a lacquered plate, and all the fruits, powdered over with frost, had a wonderful mellowness, a discrete radiance like silk-draped gold. It was all vaguely evocative of a church saint's day; the red cassocks under the lacy robes, and the gilt on a lace altar cloth....

But my most treasured memories concerning oranges come from Barbicaglia, a large garden close to Ajaccio, where I was about to have a siesta in the hottest time of the day. The orange trees were taller and further apart than in Blidah and reached down to the road, behind a ditched hedge. Immediately beyond the road, there was the deep blue sea.... I have had such happy times in that orchard. The orange trees in flower and in fruit, spread their delightful perfume around. Occasionally, a ripe orange, would fall and drop to the ground near me with a dull thud, and I just had to stretch out my hand. They were superb fruit, with their purple, blood-colour flesh inside, and looked exquisite, toning in with the surrounding stunning scenery. Between the leaves, the sea was seen in dazzling blue patches, like shattered glass sparkling in the sea mist. The ever-moving sea disturbed the atmosphere far away and caused a rhythmic murmur that soothed, like being on a boat. Oh, the heat, and the smell of oranges.... It was just so very refreshing to sleep in that orchard at Barbicaglia!

Sometimes, however, at the height of the siesta, a drum-roll would wake me up with a start. The boys of the military band came over there to practice on the road. Through the gaps in the hedge, I could see the brass decoration on the drums and the white aprons on their red trousers. The poor devils came into what little shade was offered by the hedge to hide for a while from the blinding light, pitilessly reflected from the dust on the road. And they played on until they became very, very hot! I forced myself from my dream-like state, and amused myself by throwing them some of the golden, red fruit that I could easily reach. My target drummer stopped. There was a short pause, as he looked around for the source of this superb orange rolling into the ditch beside him, before snatching it up and taking a grateful mouthful without even bothering to peel it.

Right next to Barbicaglia, over a low wall, I overlooked a small, strange garden of an Italianate design in a small plot of land. Its sand-covered paths bordered by bright green box trees and two cypress trees guarding the entrance gave it the look of a Marseille country seat. There was no shade whatsoever. At the far end, there was a white stone building with skylight windows on the ground floor. At first I thought it was a country house, but on closer inspection, I noticed a cross on the roof, and a carved inscription in the stone which I couldn't make out from here. I knew then that it was a Corsican family tomb. These little mausoleums can be seen all around Ajaccio, well-spaced, and surrounded by a garden. The families go there on Sundays, to visit their dead. A setting like that, gives death a less gloomy air than the confusion of cemeteries; and there is only the footsteps of friends to disturb the silence.

From where I was, I could see an old chap shuffling calmly around the paths. All day long, he trimmed the trees, dug the ground over, and watered and dead-headed the flowers with great care. At sunset, he went into the small chapel, where the family dead lay, to put away the spade, the rakes, and the large watering cans, while displaying all the respectful tranquillity and serenity of a cemetery gardener. The man worked with a certain subliminal reverence, and always locked the vault door quietly, as if wary of waking somebody. Within its great and glorious silence, the upkeep of this little garden troubled no one and didn't by any means depress the neighbourhood; in fact, only the immense sea and the infinite sky had more grandeur. This everlasting siesta—surrounded as it was by the overwhelming sights and forces of nature—brought a sense of eternal repose to everything in sight....

The Two Inns

I was on my way back from Nîmes, one crushingly hot afternoon in July. As far as the eye could see, the white, blistering road, was turning to clouds of dust between olive groves and small oaks, under a great, silver, hazy sun which filled the whole sky. Not a trace of shade, not a whisper of wind. Nothing except the shimmering of the hot air and the strident cry of the cicadas' incessant din, deafening, hurried, and seeming to harmonise with the immense luminous shimmering.... I had walked for two hours in this desert in the middle of nowhere, when suddenly a group of white houses emerged from the dust cloud in the road in front of me. They were known as the Saint-Vincent coaching inns: five or six farms with long red roofed barns; and a dried up watering hole in a would-be oasis of spindly fig trees. At the end of the village, two large inns faced each other across the road.

There was something striking about these inns and their strange setting. On one side, there was a large, new building, full of life and buzzing with activity. All the doors were ajar; a coach was in front, from which the steaming horses were being unhitched. The disembarked passengers were hurriedly drinking in the partial shade by the walls. There was a courtyard strewn with mules and wagons, and the wagoners were lying down under the outhouses waiting to feel cool. Inside there was the jumbled sound of shouting, swearing, fists banging on the tables, glasses clinking, billiard balls rattling, lemonade corks popping, and above all that racket, a joyful voice, bursting with song loud enough to shake the windows:

The lovely Margoton,
Just as soon as night was day,
Took her little silver can,
To the river made her away....

... The inn on the other side was silent and looked completely abandoned. There was grass under the gate, broken blinds, and a branch of dead holly on the door; all that was left of an old decoration. The entrance steps were supported by stones from the road.... It was so poor and pitiful, that it was a real act of charity to stop there at all, even for a drink.

As I went in, I saw a long gloomy, deserted room, with daylight, bursting in through three large, curtainless, windows, which just made it look even more deserted and gloomy. There were some unsteady tables, with dust-covered glasses long abandoned on them. There was also a broken billiard table which held out its six pockets like begging bowls, a yellow couch, and an old bar, all slumbering on in the heavy, unhealthy heat.

And the flies! Oh, God, the flies! I have never seen so many. They were on the ceiling, stuck to the windows, in the glasses, in clusters everywhere…. When I opened the door, there was a buzzing as if I had just entered a bee hive. At the back of the room, in a window, there was a woman standing, her face pressed against the glass and totally absorbed in looking through it. I called to her twice:

—Hello, landlady!

She turned round slowly and revealed a pitiful peasant's face, wrinkled, cracked, earth coloured, and framed in long strands of brownish lace, like old women wear hereabouts. And yet, she wasn't an old woman, perhaps the tears had wilted her.

—What can I do for you? She asked me, drying her eyes.

—Just a sit down and a drink….

She looked at me, utterly astonished, and didn't move as if she hadn't understood.

—This is an inn, isn't it?

The woman sighed:

—Yes … it's an inn, in a manner of speaking…. But why aren't you over the road like everybody else? It's a much livelier place….

—It's a bit too lively for my liking…. I'd rather stay here.

And without waiting for her reply, I sat down at a table. Once she had satisfied herself that I was genuine, she began to flit to and fro busily, opening drawers, moving bottles, wiping glasses, and flicking the flies away…. You could see that a customer was quite an event for her. Now and then the unfortunate woman would hold her head as if she was despairing of getting to the end of it.

Then she disappeared into a back room; I heard her take up some keys, fiddle with the locks, rummage in the bread bin, huff and puff, do some dusting, wash some plates. And from time to time … a muffled sob…. After a quarter of an hour of this performance, a plate of dried raisins, an old Beaucaire loaf as hard as the dish it came on, and a bottle of cheap wine, were placed before me.

—There you are, said the strange creature, and rushed back to her place at the window.

I tried to engage her in conversation as I was drinking up.

—You don't often get people here do you, madam?

— Oh, no, monsieur, never, no one…. It was very different at the time when we were the only the coaching inn around here. We did the lunches for the hunt during the soter bird season, as well as coaches all the year round…. But since the other place has opened up, we've lost everything…. The world and his wife prefer to go across the way. They find it just too miserable here…. The simple fact is that this place doesn't interest them. I'm not beautiful, I have prickly heat, and my two little girls are dead…. Over there it's very different, there is laughter all the time. A woman from Arles, a beautiful woman with lots of lace and three gold chains round her neck, keeps the place. The driver, her lover, brings in customers for her in the coach. She also has a number of attractive girls for chamber maids…. This also brings lots of business in! She gets all the young people from Bezouces, from Redessan and from Jonquières. The coachmen go out of their way to call in at her place…. As for me, I'm stuck in here all day, all alone, eating my heart out.

She said all that with a distracted, vacant way, forehead still pressed against the window pane. Obviously, there was something in the inn opposite that really interested her…. Suddenly, over the road, a lot started to happen. The coach edged forward in the dust. The sounds of cracking whips and a horn was heard. The young girls squeezed together in the doorway and shouted:

—Goodbye!… Goodbye!… And above all that, the wonderful voice, singing, as before, most beautifully,

Took her little silver can,
To the river made her way,
She didn't notice by the water,
Three young cavaliers, quite near.

The woman's whole body shook on hearing that voice; and she turned towards me and whispered:

—Do you hear that? That's my husband…. Don't you think he has a beautiful voice?

I looked at her, stupefied.

—What? Your husband?… So even he goes over there?

Then, with an apologetic air, but movingly, she said:

—What can you do, monsieur? Men are like that, they don't like tears, and I'm always breaking down, since our little girls died…. Then, this dump of a place, where nobody comes, is so miserable…. Well then, when he gets really fed up, my poor dear José goes over the road for a drink, and, the woman from Arles gets him to sing with that gorgeous voice of his. Hush!… There he goes again. And, trembling, and with huge tears that made her look even more ugly, she stood there in front of the window, hands held out in ecstasy, listening to her José singing to the woman from Arles:

The first was bold and whispered to her,
You're so beautiful my dear!

At Milianah

Notes from the Voyage.

This time, I am going to take you away to spend a day a very long way from the windmill in a pretty little Algerian town…. It will be a nice change from the tambourines and cicadas….

… There's rain in the air; the sky is grey; the crests of Mount Zaccar are enveloped in fog; it's a miserable Sunday…. I'm in my small hotel room, lighting one cigarette after another, just trying to take my mind off things…. The hotel library has been put at my disposal. I find an odd volume of Montaigne between a detailed history of hotel registrations and a few Paul de Kock novels. Opening it at random, I re-read the admirable essay on the death of La Boétie…. So, now I'm more dreamy and gloomy than ever…. A few drops of rain are starting to fall, each one leaving a large star in the dust accumulated on the windowsill since last year's rain…. The book slips out of my hands, as I stare hypnotically at the melancholy star for some time….

The town clock strikes two on an old marabout whose slender, high, white walls I can see from here…. Poor old marabout. Thirty years ago, who would have thought that one day it would have a big municipal dial stuck in its solar plexus, and on Sundays, on the stroke of two, it would give a lead to the churches of Milianah, to sound their bells for Vespers?… There they go now, ringing away…. And not for a brief spell, either…

Without doubt this room is a miserable place. The huge, dawn spinners, known as philosopher's thought spiders, have spun their webs everywhere…. I'm going out.

I'm on the main square, now. Just the place for the military band of the Third Division, not put off by a bit of rain, which has just arranged itself around the conductor. The Brigade General appears at one of the Division windows, surrounded by his fancy women. The sub-prefect is on the square and walks to and fro on the arm of the Justice of the Peace. Half a dozen young Arabs, stripped to the waist, are playing marbles in a corner to the sound of their own ferocious shouting. Elsewhere, an old Jew in rags comes to look for a ray of sunshine he left here yesterday and looks astonished not to find it…. "One, two, three…!" the band launched into an old Talexian mazurka, which Barbary organs used to play, irritatingly, under my window last year. But it moved me to tears today.

Oh, how happy are these musicians of the third! Their eyes fixed on the dotted crochets, drunk on rhythm and noise, only conscious of counting beats. Their whole being was in that hand-sized bit of paper vibrating in brass prongs at the end of their instruments. "One, two, three…!" They have everything they need these fine men, except they never play the national anthem; it makes them home sick…. Alas, I haven't much of a musical ear and this piece irritates me, so I'm off….

Now, where on earth would I be able to have a nice time, on a grey Sunday like this? I know! Sid'Omar's shop is open. I'm going there.

He may have a shop, Sid'Omar, but he is no shopkeeper. He is a prince of the blood line, the son of a former Dey of Algeria, who was strangled to death by Turkish soldiers…. When his father was killed, he sought refuge in Milianah with his adored mother. He lived there for several years like a fine gentleman philosopher with his greyhounds, falcons, horses, and wives in this attractive and refreshing palace, amongst the orange trees and fountains. Then the French came; we came. Sid'Omar was our enemy at first and allied himself with Abd-el-Kader, but then he fell out with the Emir and surrendered to us. While Sid'Omar was away from Milianah, the Emir took revenge by pillaging his palace. He flattened his orange trees, made off with his horses and wives; and killed his mother, cruelly crushing her throat under the lid of a large chest…. Sid'Omar's anger knew no bounds: within the hour he had enrolled himself in the French army, and we had no better, fiercer soldier, for as long as our war with the Emir lasted. Sid'Omar returned to Milianah; but even today at the merest mention of Abd-el-Kader, he grows pale and his eyes light up.

Sid'Omar is sixty now, and despite his age and the smallpox, his face has stayed rather handsome. He has long eyelashes, with an appealing look and a charming smile; very prince-like. The war ruined him, and all he has left of his former opulence is a farm in the plain of Chélif and a house in Milianah, where he lives a bourgeois life with his three sons, who are being brought up under his aegis. The local bigwigs hold him in some veneration. If a dispute breaks out they are only too happy to let him arbitrate; and his judgement usually carries the weight of law. He seldom goes out; you can usually find him every afternoon next door in a shop which opens onto the road. It is not opulently furnished; the walls are whitewashed, and there are a circular wooden bench, cushions, long pipes, and two braziers…. This is where Sid'Omar gives his audiences and dispenses justice. Hey! Solomon in a shop.

Today is Sunday and there is a good turn out. A dozen leaders, each in their burnous, are squatting all around the room, a large pipe and small fine filigreed eggcup full of coffee to hand. I go in; nobody moves.... From where he is, Sid'Omar gives me his most charming smile by way of a greeting and beckons me to sit next to him on a large yellow silk cushion. He puts a finger to his mouth to indicate that I should listen.

The case is between the leader of the Beni-Zougzougs and a Jew from Milianah, who are having a dispute about a plot of land. The two parties had agreed to put their differences to Sid'Omar and to abide by his judgement. The meeting is set for this very day, and the witnesses are assembled. Surprisingly, it is my Jew, and he is having second thoughts and has come alone, without witnesses, declaring that he would prefer to rely on the judgement of a French Justice of the Peace than on Sid'Omar's.... That was where things stood when I arrived.

The Jew—old, greying beard, brown jacket, blue stockings, and velvet cap—raises his eyes to the sky and rolls them, kisses Sid'Omar's silk slippers, bows his head, kneels down, and clasps his hands together, pleadingly.... I have no Arabic, but from the Jew's miming and from the words Joustees of the peace, Joustees of the peace, which he keeps repeating, I get the gist of what he is saying.

—I have no doubts about Sid'Omar, Sid'Omar is wise, Sid'Omar is just.... But, the Joustees of the Peace would be more suitable for our business.

The audience is indignant, and yet remains impassive as Arabs do.... Stretched out on his cushion, his eyes blurred, the amber book to his lips, Sid'Omar—that master of irony—smiles as he listens. Suddenly, at the height of his pleas, the Jew is interrupted by an energetic caramba! which stops him. Dead. The voice belongs to a Spanish colonial, who has come as a witness for the leader, and who then leaves his place and approaches the Judas Jew, and pours a bucketful of imprecations in all tongues and shades of blue over his head—mixed with other French expressions too gross to repeat.... Sid'Omar's son, who understands French, reddened on hearing such words in front of his father and leaves—keeping up an Arabic tradition. The audience is still impassive, Sid'Omar still smiling on. The Jew stands up and backs towards the door, trembling and scared, and babbles on about his everlasting, Joustees of the Peas, Joustees of the Peas.... He leaves. The Spaniard, furious, is at his heels and meets up with him in the road before hitting him; twice; full in the face.... the Jew falls to his knees, with his arms covering his face. The Spaniard, a little ashamed of himself, comes back into the shop.... As soon as he is safely inside, the Jew gets up with a shifty look at the motley crowd surrounding him. There were people of many races and colours there—Maltese, Minorcans, Negroes, and Arabs, all united—for once—in hating the Jew and loving to see him so maltreated.... The Jew hesitates a while, then grabs an Arab by his burnous:

—You saw him ... Achmed, you saw him ... you were there!... The Christian hit me ... you shall be a witness ... yes ... yes ... you shall be a witness.

The Arab frees his burnous and pushes the Jew away.... He knows nothing; he's seen nothing; he was looking the other way....

—How about you, Kaddour, you saw him.... You saw the Christian strike me ... shouts my unfortunate Jew to a big Negro who is impassively peeling a Barbary fig....

The Negro spits his contempt and moves away, he hasn't seen a thing. Neither has the little Maltese, whose coal-black eyes glisten viciously under his biretta; nor the rust-coloured girl from Mahon who, placing a basket of pomegranates on her head, laughs it all, and him, off....

No matter how much the Jew shouts, pleads, demeans himself ... no witnesses! Nobody saw anything.... By chance, just then a couple of fellow Zionists pass by. They are humiliated, and cower by a wall. The Jew spots them:

—Quick, quick, brothers. Quick, to the consultant! Quick to the Joustees of the Peas!... The rest of you, you saw him.... you saw him beat the old man up!

As if they'd seen him!... I don't think so.

... Things are getting lively in old Sid'Omar's shop.... The proprietor refills their cups, and relights their pipes. They chat on, and they laugh fit to burst. It's such a pleasure to see a Jew beaten up!... In the middle of the hubbub and smoke, I slip out quietly; I want to wander in the Jewish quarter, to see how my Jew's coreligionists, are taking their brother's outrage....

—Come to dinner tonight, m'sier, the good old Sid'Omar shouted....

I agree and thank him. I go outside. In the Jewish quarter, there is turmoil. The matter has already attracted a lot of attention. Nobody is minding the store. Embroiderers, tailors, and saddlers—all Israel is out on the street.... The men in their velvet caps, and blue woollen stockings fidgeting noisily in groups.... The women, pale, bloated, and unattractive in their thin dresses and gold fronts, have their faces wrapped in black bandages, and are going from group to group, caterwauling.... As I arrive, something starts to move in the crowd. There's an urgency and a crush.... Relying on their witness, my

Jew—hero of the hour—passes between two rows of caps, under a hail of exhortations:

—Revenge yourself, brother, revenge us, revenge the Jewish people. Fear nothing; you have the law on your side.

A hideous dwarf, smelling of pitch and old leather, comes to me pitifully, sighing deeply:

—You see! he said to me. We're hard done by, we Jews. How they treat us! He's an old man. Look! They've practically killed him.

It's true, my poor Jew looks more dead than alive. He goes past me—his eyes lifeless, his face haggard—not so much walking as dragging himself along…. Only a huge compensation looks likely to make him feel any better; after all, he is going to the consultant, not to the doctor.

There are almost as many consultants in Algeria as there are grasshoppers. It's a good living, I'd say. In any case, it has the great advantage that you can just walk into it, without passing examinations, or leaving a bond, or being trained. In Paris you become a lawyer; in Algeria a consultant. It's enough to have a bit of French, Spanish, and Arabian, and to have a code of conduct in your saddle bag; but above all else, you need the right temperament for the job.

The agent's functions are very varied: he can be in turn a barrister, solicitor, broker, expert, interpreter, money dealer, commissioner, and public scribe; he is the Jack of all trades of the colony. Only Harpagon has a single Jack of all trades; the rest of the colony has a surfeit, and nowhere more than Milianah, where they can be counted in dozens. Usually, to avoid office expenses, these gentlemen meet their clients in the café in the main square and give their consultations—did I say give?—between the appetiser and the after dinner wine.

The dignified Jew is making his way towards the café in the main square, with the two witnesses at his side. I will leave them to it.

As I leave the Jewish quarter, I go past the Arab Bureau. From outside, with its slate grey roof and French flag flying above, it could be taken for the village town hall. I know the interpreter, so I go in and have a cigarette with him. In between fags, this sunless Sunday has turned out quite well.

The yard in front of the Bureau is packed with shabbily dressed Arabs. Fifteen of them, in their burnouses, are squatting there along the wall, turning it into a sort of lobby. This Bedouin area—despite being in the open air—gives off a very strong smell of human flesh. Moving quickly past…. I find the interpreter occupied with two large, loud-mouthed Arabs, quite naked under their filthy blankets, madly miming some story or other about a stolen chain. I sit down on a mat in a corner and look on…. The Milianah's interpreter's uniform is very fetching, and how well he carries it! They are made for each other. The uniform is sky blue with black frogging and shiny gold buttons. With fair tightly curled hair and a light-skin, he cuts a fine figure, this hussar in blue, and is full of fun and strange tales. He is naturally talkative—he speaks many languages, and is a bit of a religious sceptic; he knew Renan at the Oriental School!—a great amateur sportsman, he is equally at ease in an Arab tent or at the Sub-prefect's soirées. He dances the mazurka as well as anyone, and makes couscous better than anyone. To sum up, he's a Parisian, and he's my sort of man. No wonder the women are mad about him…. He is a sharp dresser, and only the Arab Bureau's sergeant is in the same league, the sergeant—who, with his uniform of fine material and mother of pearl buttoned leggings, causes envy, and despair, in the garrison. Our man is on attachment to the Bureau, and he is excused fatigues and is often seen in the streets, white gloved, his hair freshly curled, and large files under his arm. He is admired and he is feared. He is authoritative.

To be sure, this story of the stolen chain threatens to become an epic. Bye-bye! I shan't wait for the end.

The Bureau area is in uproar as I leave. The crowd is crushing round a tall, pale, proud, local man dressed in a black burnous. A week ago, this man fought a panther in the Zaccar. The panther is dead; but the man has lost half his left arm. In the morning and at night he comes to have his wounds dressed at the Bureau, and every time, he is stopped in the yard and has to re-tell his story. He speaks slowly, with beautifully guttural voice. From time to time he pulls his burnous to one side and shows his left arm, strapped to his chest and wrapped in bloody blankets.

The moment I come into the street a violent storm breaks. Rain, thunder, lightning, sirocco…. Quickly, I take shelter in the first available doorway, and fall amongst a bunch of bohemians, crowded into the archways of a Moorish courtyard. It adjoins the Milianah mosque, and is a regular refuge for the Muslim destitute. They call it the Courtyard of the Poor.

Large, emaciated, lousy, and threatening, greyhounds range around me. Backed up against the gallery pillars, I try to keep control of myself and don't talk to anyone, as I try to look unconcernedly at the rain bouncing off the flagstones. The bohemians are lying about carelessly. Close by me is a young woman, almost beautiful, with her breasts and legs uncovered, and thick iron bracelets on her wrists and ankles. She is singing a strange tune consisting of three melancholic, nasal notes, while she is breast feeding a naked, reddish-bronze child, and fills a mortar with barley with her free arm. The wind-blown rain sometimes soaks the arms of the nursing woman and the body of the child. The bohemian girl completely ignores this and keeps singing during the gusts, while still piling up the barley and giving suck.

The storm abates and gives me a chance to leave the courtyard of Miracles and make my way towards dinner at Sid'Omar's, now imminent.... As I cross the main square, I run into my Jew of recent memory again. He is leaning on his consultant; his witnesses are following happily behind him, and a bunch of naughty, little Jewish boys skip around him.... They are all beaming. The consultant is taking charge of the affair; he will ask for two thousand francs compensation from the tribunal.

Dinner at Sid'Omar's is sumptuous. The dining room opens onto a Moorish courtyard, where two or three fountains are playing.... It's an excellent Turkish meal, whose highlights are poulet aux amandes, couscous à la vanille, and tortue à la viande—a bit heavy, but a gourmet meal nevertheless—and biscuits made with honey called bouchées du kadi.... For wine—nothing but champagne. Sid'Omar managed to drink some despite Muslim law—while the servers were looking away.... After dinner we go into our host's room where we are served with sweetmeats, pipes, and coffee.... The furnishings of this room are sparse: a divan, several mats, and a large high bed at the back scattered with gold embroidered red cushions.... A Turkish painting of the exploits of a certain Hamadi hangs upon the wall. Turkish painters only seem to use one colour per canvas. This canvas is decidedly green. The sea, the sky, the ships, even the admiral himself, everything is green, and deep green at that!... Arabs usually retire early, so, once I have finished my coffee and smoked my pipe, I bid goodnight to my host and leave him to his wives.

Now, where to round off my evening? Well, it's too early for bed, the spahi soldiers haven't sounded the retreat on their bugles, yet. Moreover, Sid'Omar's gold cushions were dancing fabulous farandoles round me and making sleep impossible.... I'm outside the theatre, let's go in for a moment.

The Milianah theatre is an old fur store, refurbished as far as possible to make a stage and auditorium. The lighting is made up of large oil lamps which are refilled during the interval. The audience stands; only the orchestra sits, but on benches. The galleries are quite swish with cane chairs.... All around the room there is a long, dark corridor with no wooden flooring.... You might as well be in the street, it has absolutely nothing in it. The play has already started when I arrive. The actors aren't at all bad, the men at least; they get their training from life.... They are mainly amateurs, soldiers of the third division, and the regiment is proud of them and supports them every night.

As for the women, well!... It always is and always will be the same in small provincial theatres, the women are always pretentious, artificial, and overact outrageously.... And yet, among the women there are two very young Jewesses, beginners at the drama, who catch my eye.... Their parents are in the audience and seem enchanted. They are convinced that their daughters are going to earn a fortune on the stage. The legendary Rachel, Israeli millionaire, and actress, has an orient-wide reputation with the Jews.

Nothing could be more comical and pathetic than these two little Jewesses on the boards.... They stand timidly in a corner of the scene, powdered, made-up, and as stiff as a board in low cut dresses. They are cold and they are embarrassed. Occasionally, they gabble a phrase without understanding its meaning, and as they speak, gaze vacantly into the auditorium.

I leave the theatre.... I hear shouting in the surrounding blackness from somewhere in the square.... Some Maltese settling a point, no doubt, at the point of a knife....I return slowly along the ramparts to the hotel. A gorgeous scent of oranges and thujas wafts up from the plain. The air is mild and the sky almost clear.... At the end of the road, yonder, an old, walled phantom reaches upwards—the debris of some old temple. This wall is sacred. Every day, Arab women come to hang ex-voto gifts, bits of haiks and foutas, long tresses of red hair tied with silver wire, and bits of burnous.... All this dances about in the warm breeze, lit by a narrow ray of moonlight....

The Locusts

Just one more souvenir of Algeria and then—back to the windmill!...

I couldn't sleep the night I arrived at the farm of the Sahel. Maybe it was the new country, the stress of the voyage, the barking jackals, on top of the irritating, oppressive, and completely asphyxiating heat. It felt as though the mosquito nets were keeping the air out with the insects.... As I opened my window at first light, I saw a heavy summer mist, slow-moving, fringed with black and pink, and floating in the air like smoke over a battle field. Not a leaf moved in the lovely gardens stretched out before me, where, the well-spaced vines, that gave such sweet wine, were enjoying full sunshine on the slopes. There were also European fruit trees sheltered in a shady spot, and small orange and mandarin trees in long, closely packed lines. Everything had the same gloomy look about it, with that certain limpness of leaf waiting for the storm. Even the banana trees, those great, pale-green reeds, usually on the move as some light breeze tangles their fine, light foliage, stood straight and silent in their symmetrical plumage.

I stayed there for a while looking at this fabulous plantation, where seemingly all types of the world's trees could be found, each one giving exotic flowers and fruit, in its proper season. Between the wheat fields and the massive cork-oaks, a stream shone, and refreshed—the eye at least—on an airless morning. As I approved the fineness and order of it all: the beautiful farm with its Moorish arcades and terraces, brilliantly white in the dawn, and its surrounding stables and barns, I recalled that it was twenty years since these brave settlers set up home in the valley of the Sahel. At first, they found only a workman's shack, and ground haphazardly planted with dwarf palms and mastic trees. Everything was yet to be done; everything to be built. At any time, there could be an attack from Arabs. They had to leave the plough out for cover in case of a shoot-out. Then there was the sickness, the ophthalmia, the fevers; and the failed harvest, the groping inexperience, and the fight against a narrow-minded administration—always putting off its prevarications. What a world of work, and fatigue, and having to watch their backs all the time!

Even now, despite the end of the bad times, and the hard-won good fortune, both the settler and his wife were up before anyone else on the farm. At an ungodly hour they could be heard coming and going, overlooking the workers' coffee, in the huge kitchens on the ground floor. Shortly afterwards, a bell was rung and the workmen set out for the day's work. There were some Burgundy wine-growers, Kabyle workers in rags and red tarbooshes, bare-legged Mahonian terrace workers, Maltese, and people from Lucca; men from many places and therefore more difficult to manage. Outside the door, the farmer curtly gave out the day's work to everyone. When he was finished, this fine man looked up and scrutinised the sky anxiously. Then, he noticed me at the window:

—Awful growing weather, he told me, here comes the sirocco.

In fact, as the sun rose waves of hot, suffocating air came in from the south as though an oven door had briefly opened. We didn't know where to put ourselves or what to do. The whole morning was like this. We took coffee sitting on mats in the gallery, without finding the will power to move or speak. The dogs, stretched out, hoping the flagstones would keep them cool, looked utterly washed out. Lunch picked us up a bit; it was a generous if singular meal, and included carp, trout, wild boar, hedgehog, Staouëli butter, Crescian wines, guavas, and bananas. All in all, an improbability of delicacies which nevertheless reflected the complex variety of nature which surrounded us.... We were just about to get up from the table, when shouts rang out from behind the closed French window, shouts that guaranteed that we would soon experience first-hand the furnace-like heat in the garden:

—Locusts! Locusts!

My host paled, as any man would who had been told of an impending catastrophe, and we shot outside. For ten minutes, in the farmhouse, once so calm, there was the sound of running footsteps, and indistinct voices lost in the sudden panic. From the shade of the dormitories, the servants rushed outside banging and clanging anything that came to hand; sticks, forks, flails, copper cauldrons, basins, saucepans. The shepherds blew their horns, others blew their conches or their hunting horns; a fearfully discordant racket, soon overlaid by the shrill voices of the Arab women ululating as they rushed out from nearby caves. Sometimes, setting up a great racket and a resonant vibration in the air is enough to send the locusts away, or at least to stop them coming down.

So, where were they then, these awful creatures? In a sky vibrant with heat, I saw nothing except a solitary cloud forming on the horizon, a dense, copper-coloured, hail-cloud, but making a din like a storm in a forest. It was the locusts. They flew en masse, suspended on their long, thin wings and despite all the shouting and effort, they just kept on coming, casting a huge, threatening shadow over the plain. Soon they were overhead. The edges of the cloud frayed momentarily and then broke away, as some of them, distinct and reddish, peeled off from the rest like the first few drops of a shower. Then, the whole cloud burst and a hailstorm of insects fell thick, fast, and loud. As far as the eye could see, the fields were completely obliterated by locusts. And they were enormous; each one as big as a finger.

Then the killing began to a hideous squelching sound like straw being crushed. The heaving soil was turned over using harrows, mattocks, and ploughs. But the more you killed, the more of them there were. They swarmed in waves, their front legs all tangled up, their back legs leaping for dear life—sometimes into the path of the horses harnessed up for this bizarre work. The farm dogs, and some from the caves, were released onto the fields, and fell amongst them crunching them in a frenzy. Then, two companies of Turks following their buglers came to the aid of the colonists, and the massacre changed complexion completely.

They didn't crush the locusts, they burnt them with a wide sprinkling of gunpowder.

I was drained by all this killing and sickened by the smell, so I went back into the farmhouse, but there were almost as many in there. They had come in through the open doors and windows and down the chimney. On the woodwork and curtains, already stripped, they crawled, fell, fluttered, and climbed up the white wall, casting huge shadows making them look even uglier. And there was just no getting away from the awful stench.

Later, we had to do without water with our meal as the tanks, basins, wells, and fish ponds were all covered over with dead locusts. In the evening, in my room, where many had been killed, I heard a buzzing under the furniture, and the cracking of wing cases, which sounded like plant pods bursting in the sweltering heat. Naturally, I couldn't sleep again. Besides, everybody else was still noisily busy all over the farm. Flames were spreading over the ground from one end of the plain to the other; the Turks were still in their killing fields.

The next day, opening my window, I could see that the locusts were gone. But what total devastation they left behind. There wasn't a single flower, or a blade of grass; everything was black, charred, and eaten away. Only the banana, apricot, peach, and mandarin trees could be recognised by the outline of their stripped branches, but lacking the charm and flourish of the leaves which only yesterday had been their living essence. The rooms and the water tanks were being washed out. Everywhere, labourers were digging into the ground destroying the locusts' eggs. Each sod of soil was carefully examined and turned over. But it broke their hearts to see the thousands of white, sap-filled roots in the crumbling, still-fertile soil....

Father Gaucher's Elixir

—Drink this, friend,; and tell me what you think of it.

At this, the priest of Graveson, with all the care of a jeweller counting pearls, poured me two fingers of what proved to be a fresh, golden, cordial, sparklingly exquisite liqueur.... It warmed the cockles of my heart.

—It's Father Gaucher's elixir, the pleasure and toast of Provence, crowed the kind man, it's made at the White Canons' Monastery, a few kilometres from your windmill.... Now, isn't that worth all the Chartreuses in the world?... And if you'd like to know the amusing story of this delightful elixir, listen to this....

The presbytery's dining room was genuine, and calm, with little pictures of the Stations of the Cross, and attractive, clear curtains starched like a surplice. It was in there that the priest began this short, and lightly sceptical and irreverent story, in the manner of Erasmus, but completely without art, or malicious intent.

Twenty years ago, the Norbertian monks, called the White Canons in Provence, hit some really hard times. To see their living conditions at that time was to feel their pain.

Their great wall and St. Pacôme's tower were crumbling away. The cloister was disappearing under the weeds, the columns were splitting, and the stone saints were collapsing in their niches. There was no stained glass window unbroken; nor door still on its hinges. Within the chapels and the inner cloister, the Rhone wind entered, just like in the Camargue, blowing out candles, bending the lead and breaking the glass, and skimming the holy water from its font. Tellingly sadly, the convent bell hung as silent as an empty dovecote, forcing the penniless Fathers to call to matins with an almond wood clapper!...

Oh, the woeful White Canons. I can still see them in procession on Corpus Christi day, sadly filing past in their patched capes—pale, emaciated, as befitted their mainly watermelon diet—followed by his grace the abbot, head lowered, shamed by his tarnished crosier, and his eaten away, white, wool mitre. The lady followers of the brotherhood were reduced to tears of pity in the procession, and the well-built banner-carriers were tittering quietly amongst themselves as the poor monks appeared,

—Those who dream together, starve together

The fact is that the unfortunate White Canons had come to the point where they were wondering if they wouldn't be better off finding a place in the real world with every man for himself.

One day when this grave matter was under discussion in the chapter, the prior was informed that Brother Gaucher wanted to be heard in the assembly.... Brother Gaucher was the monastery cowherd, which meant that he spent his entire day wandering around the cloister, driving two old, emaciated cows from one archway to another, to graze the grass in the gaps in the paving. He had been looked after for twelve years by an old woman from the Baux country, known as aunty Bégon, before he was taken in by the monks. The unfortunate cowherd had been unable to learn anything but how to look after his cattle and to recite his Our Father; and then only in the Provencal language, as he was too dull witted for anything else, and about as sharp as a butter-knife. Otherwise, he was a fervent Christian, although a touch extreme, at ease in a hair shirt and doing self-chastisement with commendable vigour, and, oh, brother, his strong arms!...

As he entered the chapter room, simple and uncouth, and greeted the assembly with a sort of curtsey, the Prior, Canons, Treasurer, in fact, everybody began to laugh. His greying hair, goatee beard and slightly wild eyes, always had this effect. It didn't bother Brother Gaucher, though.

—Reverend Fathers, he said meekly, as he twiddled with his rosary of olive pips, Although it's very true that empty vessels make the most noise, I want you to know that by further furrowing my already poor, furrowed brow, I think I have found a way to deliver us from our hardship.

—This is what I propose. You all know about aunty Bégon, the kind woman who looked after me when I was little. (May her soul rest in peace, the old vixen! She used to sing filthy songs after drinking.) I must tell you, Reverend Fathers, that when she was alive, she was as familiar with the herbs of the mountainside, as the old Corsican blackbird. Now, before she died, she developed a unique elixir made from several different kinds of herbs that we had gathered in the Alpilles.... All this was a long time ago, but, with the help of St. Augustine, and your permission, Father Abbot, I should, if I search thoroughly, be able to find the ingredients for this elixir. We will then only have to bottle it, and sell it at a good profit. This would allow the community to quietly fill its coffers, like our brother Trappists and ... and their liqueur, Grand Chartreu ...

Before he could finish, the Prior had stood up and leapt round his neck. The Canons shook him by the hand. But it was the treasurer, who was more moved than all the others, and respectfully kissed the edge of Brother

Gaucher's frayed hood.... Each one then went back to his seat and the chapter, still in session, elected to entrust the cows to Brother Thrasybule, so that Brother Gaucher could dedicate himself to making his elixir.

How what trials and tribulations the good Brother underwent to retrieve aunty Bégon's recipe, history doesn't tell us. But what you can be assured of, is that after only six months the White Canons' elixir was very popular. Throughout the districts of Avignon and Arles there wasn't a single farm which didn't have a store room containing a small brown earthenware bottle showing the arms of Provence, and a silver label depicting a monk in ecstasy, standing amongst the bottles of sweet wine and jars of picholine olives. The elixir sold in a big way, and the house of the White Canons soon became wealthy. St. Pacôme's tower was rebuilt. The Prior gloried in a new mitre, the church was fitted with finely worked stained glass; and in the fine filigree stone work of the bell tower, a whole range of bells, large and small, rang out their first fulsome peal on one fine Easter morning.

Brother Gaucher, the poor lay Brother, whose rustic charms, who had so enlivened the chapter, is no longer to be found there. From now on, he is known only as the Reverend Father Gaucher, a capable man of great learning. He lives apart from the many petty concerns of the cloister, locked all day in his distillery, while thirty monks scour the mountainside collecting pungent herbs for him.... The distillery was in an old unused chapel at the very bottom of the Canons' garden, and no one, not even the Prior himself, had a right of access. The innocence of the good Fathers had transformed it into a place of mystery and wonder. If, on occasion, a bold and curious young monk made use of the climbing vines to reach the rose window of the door, he would scramble down soon enough, alarmed by the sight of Father Gaucher, who looked like a bearded magician, leaning over his flames, holding his elixir-strength-gauge. All around, there were pink stoneware retorts, huge stills, coiled glass condensers, and all sorts of bizarre equipment, which gleamed eerily in the red light from the stained glass windows....

At nightfall, as the last angelus bell was ringing, the door of this mysterious place silently opened, and the Reverend Father Gaucher emerged to attend the evening church service. It warmed the heart to see him greeted with such joy as he crossed the monastery grounds. The brothers rushed to be at his side. They said:

—Hush! That's the Father with his secret!...

The Treasurer used to join him and spoke to him humbly....

With these adulations ringing in his ears, the Father walked on, mopping his brow, and placed his wide brimmed tricorne hat on the back of his head, where it gave all the appearance of a halo, and looked complacently around at the great courtyard planted with orange trees, and the new working weathercocks on the blue roofs. In the sparklingly white cloister—between the elegant columns decorated with flowers—the Canons, in new clothes, were filing past in pairs, in renewed health and well-being.

—It's thanks to me they can enjoy all that! the Reverend thought; and each time he did, he flushed with pride.

But, the unfortunate man was to be well punished for his pride, as you will see....

Who would have thought, that one evening, during the service, he would come to church in an extraordinarily agitated state: red-faced, out of breath, his cowl askew, and so beside himself, that as he took the holy water, he wet his sleeves up to the elbow. At first, it was thought it was the embarrassment of coming late, but he was then seen bowing deeply to the organ and the gallery instead of genuflecting to the high altar, and then breezing quickly across the church, and wandering about for five minutes looking for his stall. After all this, once seated, he turned to right and left, smiling beatifically, prompting a murmur of astonishment that spread down the three naves. From prayer book to prayer book the whisper went,

—What on earth is the matter with Father Gaucher?... What's wrong with Father Gaucher?

Twice, the Prior struck his crosier impatiently on the flagstones to command silence.... Over at the back of the choir, the psalms were still echoing out, but without any responses....

Suddenly, right in the middle of the Ave Verum, Father Gaucher slumped back into his stall and began singing in a piercing voice:

In Paris, there was a White Canon,
Who went all the way with a black nun....

This caused everyone great dismay, and they all stood up. Somebody said:

—Take him out ... he's possessed!

The Canons crossed themselves. His Grace's crosier was clattering madly away.... But Father Gaucher, was oblivious to all this; and two monks were obliged to carry him out through the little choir door, struggling as if he were being exorcised, and continuing with his hmm ... tune....

Very early the next day, the unhappy Father was in the Prior's oratory on his knees, in floods of tears, showing his contrition:

—It's the elixir, your Grace, which caught me out, he said, striking his chest. The good Prior himself was very moved to see him so grieved and penitent.

—Come, come, Father Gaucher, calm down. All this will disappear like dew in the sunshine.... After all, worse things happen at sea. Lots of people begin to sing when they are a little... hmm, hmm! We must hope that novices wouldn't have understood it.... For the moment, let's see, tell me just how this thing came to pass.... You were trying out the liqueur, weren't you? You were perhaps a little generous with your measure.... Yes, yes, I understand.... It's just like Brother Schwartz, the inventor of gunpowder: you succumbed to your own invention.... Tell me, my dear friend, is it really necessary to test this terrific liqueur on yourself?

—Alas, yes your Grace ... the elixir-strength-gauge tells me the degree of the alcohol, but for the smoothness of the finished product, I can trust nothing but my own palate....

—Oh yes, that's right ... but if I might press you a little further ... when you taste the elixir in that way, does it seem good to you? Is it enjoyable?...

—Yes, I'm afraid it does your Grace, admitted the miserable Father, flushing.... For two nights now, I found it had such a bouquet, such an aroma!... The devil himself has played this dirty trick on me.... From now on, I am determined only to try it by means of the elixir-strength-gauge. Never mind if the liqueur is not good enough, and if it isn't quite a diamond of a drink....

—Hold it right there, interrupted the Prior, sharply, We must not risk upsetting the customers.... All you need to do for the moment, as a precaution, is to keep a eye on yourself.... Let's see, how much does it take to fully establish the quality?... Lets say twenty drops.... It would need a hell of a devil to catch you out with just twenty drops.... Moreover, to avoid any possibility of accident, I am giving you a dispensation not to have to come to church. You can have a private evening service in the distillery.... And now, you may go in peace, Reverend, but ... be sure to count the drops.

Unfortunately, it was no use counting the drops.... The demon held of him anyway, and having held him, wouldn't let go.

So, now it was the distillery that heard the unusual service!

In the daytime all went well ... for a while. The Father was quite relaxed: he prepared the stoves, the stills, and carefully selected the herbs, fine, grey, dentate, the very scented essence of Provencal sunshine…. But in the evening while the basic ingredients were infusing and the elixir was cooling down in the large red coppers, the poor man's torture began.

—… Seventeen … eighteen … nineteen … twenty!…

The drops fell tantalisingly from the pipette into the silver-gilt goblet. These twenty, the Father swallowed in one go, almost without tasting them. Oh! How he would have loved to drink the health of that twenty first drop! To escape temptation, he had to lose himself in prayer kneeling at the far end of the laboratory. Unfortunately, the still warm liqueur was still releasing a hint of aromatic fumes, which swirled around him, and led him on regardless towards the vats…. The liqueur was of such a lovely golden green colour…. Poised above it, his nostrils aquiver, he stirred it very gently with his pipette, and in the twinkling eddies, which were spreading throughout the emerald ambrosia, he thought he saw the sparkling, laughing eyes of aunty Bégon looking back at him….

—Oh! Alright! Just one more drop!

One drop, yes. And then another. And another, and another, and another, until his goblet almost overflowed. By now, his struggle was over, and he collapsed into a large armchair, his body cast off, his eyelids half closed, in pleasure—and in pain—as he continued to sip his sinful cup and said with sweet remorse:

—Oh! I'm damned if I do…. I'm damned if I don't….

But the worst was still to come. As he reached the end of the diabolical liqueur, he recalled, by who knows what spell, some of the dirty songs of aunty Bégon: In Paris there was a White Canon … and so on….

Imagine the fuss the next day, when his neighbouring cell mates joked to him knowingly:

—Hey! Hey! Father Gaucher, you were well off your head last night when you went to bed.

It all ended in tears, recriminations, fasting, the hair shirt, and chastisement, of course. But nothing, nothing could defeat the demon of the drink, and every evening, at the same time, the same story.

Meanwhile, the orders were flooding into the abbey, and it was a blessing. They came from Nîmes, Aix, Avignon, Marseilles…. Day by day the monastery was gradually turning into a factory. There were Brother packers, Brother labellers, Brother accountants, and even Brother wagoners. The service to the Lord, though, was getting well and truly lost, despite the odd peal of bells. But, I can reveal to you that the poor folk of the area weren't losing out by it....

And then, one fine Sunday morning, as the Treasurer was reading out his end of year report before the whole chapter, and the good Brothers, wide eyed and smiling, were listening, Father Gaucher rushed into the meeting shouting:

—It's all over.... I am doing no more.... I want my cows back.

—So what's wrong, Father Gaucher? asked the Prior, who could well imagine something of what was wrong.

—What is wrong, your Grace?... What is wrong is that I am making an eternity of hell fire and forks for myself.... It is wrong that I am drinking, and I am drinking like a sot....

—But I told you to count the drops.

—Oh! Yes, of course, count the drops! Actually, I count by tumblers these days.... Yes, Reverends, that's how bad things are. Three flagons every evening.... You must understand that this can't continue.... Have the elixir made by whomever you choose.... But, may I burn in God-sent fire, if I have anything more to do with it.

This sobered up the chapter, at least.

—But, wretched man, you will ruin us! the treasurer shouted, brandishing his account book.

—Would you rather that I am damned?

With that the Prior stood up:

—Reverends, he said, stretching out his elegant white hand with its shining pastoral ring, there is a way to settle this.... It's in the evening, isn't it, my dear son, when the demon tempts you?...

—Yes, Prior, regularly every evening.... As well as that, as the night approaches, I get, begging your pardon, the sweats, which grip me just like Capitou's ass when he sees them coming to saddle him.

—Well then, let me reassure you.... Henceforth, every evening, during the service, we will say, for your benefit, the prayer of St. Augustine, to which a plenary indulgence is attached.... After that, you are covered no matter what happens.... It brings absolution during the actual commission of the sin.

—Oh that's really excellent! Thank you so much, Prior!

And without asking for more, Father Gaucher went happily back to his stills, walking on air.

Actually, from that moment, every evening, at the end of the last service of the day, the celebrant never forgot to add:

—Let us pray for our unfortunate Father Gaucher, who is sacrificing his soul for the benefit of the community.... Pray for us, Lord....

And while, on all the white hoods of the Brothers, prostrated in the shade of the naves, the prayer fluttered like a slight breeze on snow, elsewhere, at the back of the monastery, behind the flickering reddened glass of the distillery, Father Gaucher could be heard singing at the top of his voice,

In Paris, there was a White Canon,
Who went all the way with a black nun....

... Here, the good priest paused, horrified:

—Mercy me! If my parishioners could only hear me!

In the Camargue

DEPARTURE

There is a huge buzzing at the chateau. The messenger has just brought word from the keeper, half in French and half in Provencal, announcing that there had already been two or three fine flights of herons, and water-fowl, and that the season's first birds weren't in short supply.

"You're coming hunting with us", my friendly neighbours wrote to me; and this morning, at the unearthly hour of five o'clock, their large wagon, loaded with rifles, dogs, and provisions, came to pick me up at the bottom of the hill. Off we go on the road to Arles, which is a bit dry and the trees have mostly lost their leaves by this time in December. The pale green shoots of the olive trees are hardly visible, and the garish green of the oaks is a bit too wintry and artificial. The stables are beginning to stir into life, while very early risers light up the windows in the farms before day break. In the gaps in the stones amongst the ruins of Mont-Majeur abbey, the sea eagles, still drowsy, stretch their wings. Despite the hour, the old peasant women are coming from the Ville-de-Beaux, trotting along in their donkey carts. We pass them alongside the ditches. They have to go six country kilometres to sit on the steps of St. Trophyme to sell their small packets of medicinal herbs collected on the mountain....

The low, crenellated ramparts of Arles appear, just as you see them on old engravings, which show warriors with lances larger than the talus they are standing on. We gallop through this marvellous, small town, surely one of the most picturesque in France, with its rounded sculptured, moucharaby-like balconies, jutting out into the middle of the narrow streets. There are old black houses with tiny doors, in the Moorish style, gothic and low-roofed, which take you back to the time of William the Short-Nose and the Saracens. At this hour there's nobody about yet, except the quay on the River Rhone. The Camargue boat is steaming up at the bottom of the steps and is ready to sail. The tenant farmers are there in their red serge jackets. So are some young women of La Roquette, out looking for farm work, and standing on the deck amongst us, chatting and laughing, with their long brown mantles turned down because of the sharp morning air. The tall Arles' headdresses makes their heads look small and elegant with an attractive pertness, and they feel the need to stand on tip toe, so that their laughter and banter can be heard by everybody. The bell rings and off we go. What with the fast flow of the Rhone, the propeller, and the mistral, the two river banks speed by. On one side, there is the Crau, an arid, stony plain. On the other we have the Camargue, much greener, with its short grass and swamps full of reeds stretching all the way to the sea.

From time to time the boat pulls in at a landing stage, on the right or left bank, or on the Empire or the Kingdom, as it was known in the middle ages, in the time when Arles was a Kingdom. The old Rhone sailors still use these same words today. At every stop there was a white farm, and a clump of trees. The workmen getting off with their tools, and the women with their baskets under their arms, go straight onto the gangway. Little by little the boat empties, first on the Empire side and then on the Kingdom, and by the time we get off at Mas-de-Giraud, there's hardly anybody left on board.

The Mas-de-Giraud is an old farm of the Lords of Barbentane, and we went in to await the keeper appointed to come and meet us. In the main kitchen, all the farm hands, ploughmen, winegrowers, and shepherds are sitting at the table, solemnly, silently, and slowly eating their meal and being served by the women who have to wait to eat until the men are finished. Presently the keeper arrives with the cart. He is a real Fennimore-Cooper type, a trapper on land and water, fish-warden, and gamekeeper, known locally as the Stalker, because he can always be found in the morning mists or at nightfall stalking amongst the reeds, or stock still in his small boat watching over his keep nets on the open water and the irrigation channels. It may be this work of perpetual lookout that makes him so silent and focussed. And yet, as the cart full of rifles and baskets trundles along in front of us, he gives us news of the hunt, the number of over-flights, and the location where the birds of passage have been brought down. As he talks, he melts into the landscape.

The cultivated earth gives way to the true, untamed Camargue, amongst the pasture and the marshland, and the irrigation channels shine in amongst the goose-foot plants as far as the eye can see. Bunches of tamarisks and reeds form little islands on a calm sea. There are no tall trees; the immense evenness of the plain is unbroken. The animal sheds have roofs that slope down almost to ground level. The roaming flocks, lying in the salt grass or making their way as they nuzzle around the shepherd's red cape, don't disturb the landscape's regular flow, dwarfed, as they are, by the endless space of blue horizons and open sky. Just as a rough sea is still the sea, so a sense of solitude and immensity emerges, heightened by the relentless mistral, which, with its powerful breath, seems to flatten yet enlarge the landscape. Everything bows down before it. The smallest shrubs bear the imprint of its passage, and stay twisted and bent over southwards in an attitude of perpetual flight....

II

THE SHACK.

The roof and walls consist of dried, yellowing, reeds. This is the shack, which is to be our meeting place for the hunt. A not untypical house of the Camargue, it has a single, vast, high room with no window, getting its daylight through a glass door kept fully shuttered at night. All along the huge, rendered, whitewashed walls, the gun-rack waits for the rifles, the game bags, and the wading boots. At the back, five or six bunks are placed round an actual boat mast which is stepped into the soil and reaches the roof which it supports. During the night, while the mistral is blowing and the house is creaking everywhere, the distant sea seems nearer than it is, its sound carried by the freshening wind, and gives us the impression of being in a boat's cabin.

In the afternoon, the shack is especially charming. Throughout our beautiful, southern winter days, I enjoy being alone by the tall mantelpiece, while several twigs of tamarisk smoke away in the hearth. The howling mistral or tramontana makes the doors bang, the reeds scream, and a range of noises that make the great, natural clamour all around. The rays of the winter sun gather and are then scattered by the fierce wind. Great shadows race around under a perfect blue sky. The light comes in flashes, and the noise in crashes, and the flock's bells are suddenly heard, then lost in the wind, only to emerge again under the rattling door like a charming refrain.... Twilight, just before the hunters come back, is the most exquisite time of day. By then the wind has moderated. I go out for a moment; the great red sun, at peace at last, goes down in flames, but without heat. Night falls and brushes you with its damp, black wing as it passes over. Somewhere, at ground level, there is a bang, a flash, as the red star of a rifle shot bursts into the surrounding blackness. What is left of the day rushes past. A long flight of ducks flies by, low, as if looking for somewhere to land; but suddenly, catching sight of the cabin where the fire is lit, they take fright. The one at the head rises, and the rest follow as they fly away screaming.

Soon afterwards, a great shuffling sound, something like rain falling, approaches. Thousands of sheep, brought back by the shepherds and urged on by the dogs, are anxiously and haphazardly and breathlessly scurrying about towards the folds. I am overrun by them and they barge into me as I am caught up in a maelstrom of woollen curls, and bleating. It was an ocean swell of sheep that seems to carry away the shepherds on leaping waves of wool....

Behind the flock, friendly footsteps and joyful voices are heard. The shack fills up, and becomes lively, and boisterous. The kindling blazes on the fire. The more tired they are; the more they laugh. It is a dizzy, happy fatigue, their rifles stacked in a corner, long boots strewn about, and game bags emptied into a bloodied heap of red, golden, green, and silver plumage. In the smoke, the table is set out with a good eel soup. Silence falls; the huge silence of robust appetites; only broken by the ferocious growling of the dogs as they scuffle to sample their bowls by the door....

The evening will soon end. By now, there is only the keeper and I in front of the flickering fire. We chat desultorily, occasionally throwing half-words at each other, peasant-like, with Red Indian style grunts, which fizzle out like the last sparks of the dying fire. Eventually, the keeper stands up, lights his lantern, and I hear his heavy footsteps fade into the night....

III
THE WISH-AND-WAIT!

The wish-and-wait!, what an appropriate name for the lookout, the expectancy of the hunter lying in wait, and the uncertainty of hours of total concentration, waiting and wishing between day and night. The morning lookout is just before sunrise. There is a lookout posted from evening until twilight, which is the one I prefer, especially in this marshland where the swamp water sustains the daylight for so long....

Sometimes the lookout takes place in a tiny, punt, a narrow, keelless boat, which rolls at the drop of a hat. Hidden to peak of his cap by the reeds, the hunter, lying on the bottom of the boat, keeps an eye out for ducks. The gun barrel and the dog's head sniff the air. The dog catches mosquitoes or else stretches out its huge paws and pitches the whole shooting-match over and fills it with water. All this looking out is a bit too complicated for my tyro's taste. Most of the time, I go to the wish-and-wait on foot, paddling deep into the swamp in enormous leather waders. I move slowly and carefully for fear of getting stuck in the mud. I try to avoid stinking reeds and jumping frogs....

Happily, an islet of tamarisks finally appears and I can get myself onto some dry land. The keeper did me the honour of leaving his dog with me, a huge Great Pyrenees with a long, white, shaggy coat, a prime hunter and fishing dog, whose presence never ceases to intimidate me somewhat. When a water fowl comes within firing range, the dog has an ironical way of looking at me and throwing his head back like a disdainful arty type, and with his two long ears flopping in front of his eyes, he freezes, and wags his tail, in a perfect mime of impatience, as if to say:

—Shoot... go on then, shoot!

I obey. I miss. So, he lies down full length, and yawns and stretches himself out giving the appearance, for all the world, of being tired, discouraged, and insolent....

Oh! Very well, then, you're right, I am a bad shot. What really fascinates me about the lookout is the sunset; the dimming light taking refuge in the water of the shining lakes, which transform the grey tint of the overcast sky into a fine shade of polished silver. I love the smell of the water, and the mysterious rustling of long leaves and insects in the reeds. Every so often, a darker note sounds and rolls across the sky like the sound of a conch shell. It's the boom of the bittern as it plunges its huge, wader's beak to the bed of the swamp.... Noisy crane flights startle me and I can hear the movement of their feathered, plumed wings. Then—nothing. It's the night, the deep, dark night, with just a glimmer of daylight left lingering on the water....

Suddenly, I feel sort of nervous unease, as if someone was behind me. I turn round and am reassured by the sight of that ubiquitous travelling companion of fine nights, the moon; a low, large, and full moon rising calmly and with a visible motion which slows gradually as it rises above the horizon.

A moonlit patch is already clearly visible nearby, then another, then one further off.... Eventually the whole marsh is bathed in moonlight, and the least tuft of grass gives a shadow. The lookout is over, the birds can see us—we have to return to base. We walk bathed in a dusting of weak, blue light; each step we make in the open water and the irrigation channels stirs the horde of reflected stars and the moonlight that penetrates the depths of the water.

IV

RED AND WHITE.

Within rifle range of the shack, there is another one similar, but more rustic. It's home to our keeper, his wife and their two eldest children. The girl is responsible for the men's meal, and doing repairs to the fishing nets, while the boy helps his father look into the keep nets, and maintain the sluice gates in the ponds. The two youngest children are in Arles, staying with their grandmother, until they have learned to read and have taken their first communion. It is too far to the school and the church from here, and the atmosphere of the Camargue is completely unsuitable for young children. The fact is that, come the summer, when the marshes are dry and the white mud of the irrigation channels cracks in the great heat, the islet isn't really habitable at all.

I experienced it once when I came in August to hunt ducklings and I will never forget the miserable and ferocious appearance of the burningly hot landscape. Here and there ponds were steaming in the sun like huge fermentation vats, keeping scant signs of life, perhaps just salamanders, spiders, and water insects looking for some moisture. There was a pestilential air about, a miasmic, brooding fog thickened by innumerable clouds of mosquitoes. At the keeper's house everybody had the shivers, everybody had the fever, and it was pitiful to see the yellowed, drawn faces, and the circled, popping eyes, of these unfortunates, who were condemned to drag themselves around for three months under this high, pitiless sun, which burnt, but didn't warm…. The life of a gamekeeper is miserable and hard in the Camargue. At least ours has his wife and children round him; but a little further on in the marsh, a horse-warden lives absolutely alone, from one year's end to the next, Robinson Crusoe like. In his home-made reed cabin, there isn't a single household utensil not made by him; the woven wicker-work hammock, the three black stones that form the hearth, the tamarisk roots made into stools, even the lock and key made from white wood that secures this unique accommodation.

The man himself is at least as strange as his dwelling. He is a sort of silent thinker like so many solitary people, hiding his peasant's wariness under thick bushy eyebrows. When not on the pasture land, he can be found sitting outside his door, and with touching, childlike, care, slowly fathoming out one of the little coloured leaflets which are wrapped around phials of medicines for his horses. The poor devil hasn't any recreation but reading these leaflets. Despite being neighbours, our keeper and he don't see each other. They actually avoid each other. One day when I asked the stalker the reason for this, he replied in a serious manner:

—It's because of a difference of opinion…. He is a red; I am a white.

Well, even in this wilderness, where solitude ought to have brought them close together, these two unsociable people, as ignorant and naïve as each other, these two cowherds of Theocritus, who barely go to town once a year, and the small cafés of Arles must seem like the Palace of Ptolemy to them, have managed to fall out about politics of all things.

V
LAKE VACCARES

One of the finest sights in the Camargue is lake Vaccares. I often leave the hunt to sit down by the shore of this beautiful, brackish lake, this baby inland sea, which seems a true daughter of the ocean. Being locked indoors, so to speak, she is made all the more appealing through her captivity. There is none of the dryness and aridity that often bedevils the seaside, around our Vaccares. On its high banks, it boasts a fulsome covering of fine, velvet-smooth grass, a perfect showcase for unique and charming flora. There are centauries, clover, gentians, and those lovely flowers that are blue in winter, and red in summer, apparently changing their clothes to suit the weather, and, when they have an uninterrupted flowering season, show their full range of colours.

About five o'clock in the evening, as the sun is going down, these three watery delights, without boat and sail to cover and change them, open out into an amazing scene. No longer is it just the intimate charm of the open-water and the irrigation channels appearing here and there between folds of marl, where the smell of water pervades, and is likely to emerge at the least depression in the ground. Here, lake Vaccares gives an impression of size and space. The radiant waves attract flights of scoter ducks from far away, and herons, bitterns, and white-flanked, pink-winged flamingos, lining up to fish all along the banks, in many-coloured strands. Then there are ibis, the sacred ibis of Egypt, truly at home in this splendid sunshine and silent landscape. From where I am, I can hear nothing but the lapping of water and the ranger calling his horses from around the lakeside. Each animal on hearing its name, rushes in, mane flowing in the wind, and takes hay from his hand....

Further on, still on the same bank, there is a herd of beef cattle free ranging like the horses. Sometimes, I notice their bony, curved backs hunched over a clump of tamarisk, and their small, immature horns just visible. Most of these Camargue cattle are bred to run in the branding fêtes in the villages, and some of them are already famed in the circuses of Provence and Languedoc. In one herd of the neighbourhood, there was a terrible fighter amongst them called the Roman, who has been the undoing of I don't know how many men and horses at the bullfights at Arles, Nîmes, and Tarascon. His companions also made him the leader, for in these strange herds the animals organise themselves around an old bull which they adopt as their leader. When there is a storm on the Camargue, it is truly terrifying on the great plain, where there is nothing to divert or stop it. It's an amazing sight to see the herd group themselves behind their leader, all their heads down and turned into the wind, their whole strength behind their foreheads. Shepherds in Provence call this manoeuvre: turning the horn to wind.

Perish the herd that doesn't do it. Blinded by the rain, and carried away by the storm, the herd turns in on itself, becomes panicky, scatters, and is overwhelmed. To escape the storm, they have been known to dash headlong into the Rhone, the Vaccares, or even the sea.

Nostalgia for the Barracks and Paris.

This morning, at first light, a formidable drum-roll woke me with a start....

A drum-roll from amongst my pines at this hour!... What a ridiculous thing. For goodness sake.

As quickly as I can, I jump out of bed and run to the door.

Nobody about! The noise has ceased.... From the midst of some wet wild vines, a couple of curlews fly off noisily.... A light breeze sings in the trees.... Towards the east, on the sharp ridge of the Alpilles, a golden dust amasses, from which the sun slowly appears.... The day's first sunbeam is already touching the roof of the windmill. Immediately, the drum-roll starts again, hidden, this time from in the fields....

The devil, I had forgotten about it. What sort of idiot, then, greets the day from the middle of the woods with a drum?... I try my best to get a look, but I can't see anyone.... Nothing except the tufts of lavender and the pine trees which go down right to the road.... Perhaps there is some goblin, hidden in the thicket, mocking me.... It must be Ariel or Puck. The rascal must have said to himself as he passed my windmill:

—That Parisian is much too tranquil in there, let's have a dawn serenade for him.

Whereupon, he took up his big drum and ... more drum-rolls.... Will you shut that thing up, Puck, you will wake up the cicadas.

It wasn't Puck.

It was Gouget Francois, called Pistolet, drummer in the 31st Battalion, and right now on his biannual leave. Pistolet is bored stiff here and he has his memories, and he has his drum, and—when someone from the village wants to borrow the instrument—he goes out and bangs the damned drum in the woods, and dreams of the Prince-Eugène barracks, back in Paris.

Today, he is honouring a small, green hillock with his reveries. There he is, propping up a pine tree, his drum in his arms, having a field day.... Partridges, alarmed, take to the air from under his feet; but he doesn't notice them. Wild flowers bathe him in their scent; but he doesn't smell them.

He doesn't see the fine spiders' webs vibrating in the sun amongst the branches, nor the pine needles, which jump about on his drum. Completely given over to his reverie and his music, he looks lovingly at the blur of his whizzing drumsticks, and his large, dull face lights up with pleasure at every roll.

"How lovely the great barracks is, with its large flagged courtyard, its orderly, all in line windows, its men in military caps, and its low arcades full of clattering mess-tins!...

"Oh, the echoing steps, the whitewashed corridors, the smelly dormitory, the belts to be polished, the slab of bread, the tins of polish, the iron bedsteads with grey covers, the gleaming rifles in the rack.

"Oh, the good days with the corps, the cards that stick to your fingers, the hideous queen of spades with her feathered charms, the old newspaper, pages missing, scattered on the beds....

"Oh, the long nights on guard at the Ministry's door, the old sentry box which rains in, the frozen feet!... The carriages which splash you going past!... Oh, the extra fatigues, the days without break, the stinking wash tub, the wooden pillow, the reveille on cold, wet mornings, the retreat in fog and at lights on time, the evening call-out that finds you late and breathless!

"Oh, the bois de Vincennes, the thick, white, cotton gloves, the walks on the fortifications.... Oh, the Military School entrance, the loose women, the sound of the cornet at the Salon de Mars, the absinth in the bars, the shared secrets between hiccoughs, the sabres drawn, the sentimental tale told hand on heart...."

Dream on, poor man! I won't be the one to stop you.... Hit your drum and hit it hard, hit it as hard as you can. I have no right to ridicule you.

So, you are nostalgic for your barracks; am I not just as nostalgic for mine?

My Paris haunts me just like yours. You—you play your drum among the pines. Me—I write here.... What a right pair of Provencal people we are. Back in Paris, we miss our Alpilles and the smell of wild lavender. Right here and right now, bang in the middle of Provence, we miss our barracks, and everything that reminds us of it is so dear to us!...

Eight o'clock strikes in the village. Pistolet, drumsticks at the ready, starts on his way back.... He can be heard, playing non-stop, coming down from the woods.... Me—I lie down in the grass, overwhelmed with nostalgia. As the drum fades into the distance, All my own familiar Paris passes before my eyes, there amongst the pines....

Ah, Paris!... Paris!... Paris for ever!

CPSIA information can be obtained at www.ICGtesting.com
Printed in the USA
BVOW05s1350210416

444903BV00003B/138/P